ALCHEMY AND THE POET
THE CASE OF NOVALIS'S *HEINRICH VON OFTERDINGEN*

This study revisits Novalis's novel *Heinrich von Ofterdingen* (1802) and proposes an alchemical reading of the text. The structure and imagination of the novel evoke the journey of an initiate into mysteries, in this case the mysteries of poetry, with its magical and Orphic dimensions. This study aims to systematize a reading that connects the alchemical process with the development of the characters, offering a new understanding of the role of alchemy in the construction of the novel. The book contextualizes Novalis's thought within the Romantic movement and alchemical philosophy, tracing hermetic and mystical influences throughout his intellectual trajectory. In essence, the study argues that Novalis's work, beyond being a Romantic manifesto, is also a profound reflection on alchemy as a tool for the transformation of both self and reality. It concludes that, while alchemy is not the sole key to interpreting the novel, it provides a fertile and rich perspective for understanding both Novalis's writing and the renewed significance of alchemy in contemporary cultural, literary and philosophical studies.

ALCHEMY AND THE POET

THE CASE OF NOVALIS'S *HEINRICH VON OFTERDINGEN*

Sérgio das Neves

Critical, Cultural and Communications Press
London
2025

Alchemy and the Poet: The Case of Novalis's Heinrich von Ofterdingen
by Sérgio das Neves

Published by Critical, Cultural and Communications Press, 2025.

ISBN 9781905510771

TABLE OF CONTENTS

PREFACE Claudia J. Fischer   7

ACKNOWLEDGMENTS   9

INTRODUCTION   11

1. AN INCURABLE ROMANTIC   15
   1.1 SOME IDEALISTIC LINES AND CHALLENGES   15
   1.2. PIETISM: FAITH AND THE VALUE OF THE SELF   20
   1.3. LOVE AND KNOWLEDGE: THE SECRET LANGUAGE   25
      OF ALCHEMY
      1.3.1. JACOB BÖHME AND THE PIETISTS   30
      1.3.2. NOVALIS AND THE ALCHEMICAL MEANDERS   37
      1.3.3. THE BLUE FLOWER   45

2. HEINRICH, THE ALCHEMIST POET   52
   2.1. DREAMS AND THE YEARNING FOR THE WORK   59
   2.2. THE JOURNEY: THE BEGINNING OF THE WORK   74
   2.3. SOUND, THE CONDUCTOR OF THE WORK   93
   2.4. MÄRCHEN: A MODEL OF WORK   98
   2.5. THE WORK SUPPLANTS REALITY   113

THE WORK CONTINUES   134

REFERENCES   149

PREFACE
Claudia J. Fischer

Like many major works, this book found its genesis in the seed of a humble dream, growing into a keen curiosity, nurtured by a steady pursuit. In this instance, one might say that it began with the desire to learn a new language—a mysterious code concealing new realms of knowledge and literary pleasure to be unveiled.

When I first met Sérgio das Neves in 2014, he was a young B.A. student of Performing Arts Studies at the University of Lisbon and had just enrolled in a beginner's German language course I was teaching. Though entirely new to the language, he immediately demonstrated remarkable enthusiasm and dedication to mastering it. Over the following years, I had the privilege of observing his academic journey, noting his focused and rigorous approach to both his studies and creative endeavours. In 2018, Neves joined the Master's program in Comparative Studies and asked me to supervise his thesis centered on Goethe's *Urfaust* and Novalis's *Heinrich von Ofterdingen*. I was thrilled to see how his passion for the German language had developed into an ambitious exploration of German literature. By that time, he was thoroughly prepared to delve into the works of Classical German authors in their original language and to uncover their intriguing connections to alchemical traditions—a theme deeply embedded in German literary heritage.

Unfolding as a rich and engaging dialogue throughout the year of preparation, the thesis drew unanimous praise from the jury for its innovative perspectives on the works analysed. However, soon after, Neves felt the need, quoting his own words about this book now freshly

7

published, "to revisit the laboratories and mines". Fully dedicated to Novalis, this work allowed him to deepen even further his reading of *Heinrich von Ofterdingen* in the light of alchemical thought.

While Goethe's Faustian figures are widely recognised as closely linked to alchemical practices and have been extensively discussed in scholarly literature, this link is less immediately apparent in Novalis's novel. However, as Neves argues in this book, it is deeply and intrinsically woven into the fabric of Novalis's narrative. Neves demonstrates that the progression of Heinrich's journey—here understood as an initiation process—the prominence of the blue flower, and the structural composition of the novel itself reflect parallels with alchemical processes. These connections, often overshadowed in literary criticism by the emphasis on Romantic ideals and symbolism, reveal a deeper layer of interpretation within the text.

The alchemical *topos* of a secret language that requires a non-literal reading finds resonance in Neves's approach as well. It invites a fresh interpretation of this celebrated Romantic novel, while more broadly underscoring the inherent kinship between the poet and the alchemist, both of whom seek to transform and transcend the ordinary through knowledge and beauty. Starting with the first step, which in Novalis's terms ought to be an "inward gaze", followed by "an effective gaze outward" (1945b: 13-5) as second step, their journey of transformation is endless.

ACKNOWLEDGMENTS

I begin by expressing my gratitude to Professor Claudia J. Fischer, who readily agreed to supervise my Master's dissertation. She also graciously revisited the work to write its Preface. I am deeply thankful for her shared enthusiasm, her incisive reading, precise observations, critiques, and suggestions. It is a privilege to work with the very first German professor I encountered during my undergraduate studies at the Faculty of Arts of the University of Lisbon, eleven years ago.

I also extend my thanks to the German professors who continued to nurture my interest in the German language, literature, and culture: Vera Lemos, Nora Heitmann, Andrea Riedel, Martina Merklin, and Jasmin Mbambo. It is thanks to their dedicated efforts that I can read words, many of which remain untranslated into other languages.

I am also grateful to Professor Golgona Anghel, who is currently supervising my doctoral research, for encouraging the creation of this book. Her guidance and friendship, which transcend the boundaries of the doctoral thesis, are marked by immense generosity, openness, and critical insight. Thanks to her curiosity and strength, learning becomes an unending process.

To Francesca, I owe my gratitude for her enduring and profound friendship. This project has been enriched by Francesca's unforgettable gaze and attentive listening, and this book was no exception. It remains a great joy to continue walking alongside her.

To Professor Stephan Matthias Fröhder, I am grateful for friendship and all the support he offered during my time at Goethe University, in Frankfurt.

I extend my thanks to Professors Anabela Mendes, Fernando

Guerreiro, Yvette Centeno, and José Eduardo dos Reis for their invaluable materials, insightful words of guidance, and effective questions.

To Olinda Kleiman, Manuel Romão, Carlotta Defenu, Margarida Fialho, Kalee Prendergast, Alexandra Faustino, Amândio Reis, Edilson Galdino, and so many others who are family: as many names as those of the Philosopher's Stone, which, despite its multiplicity, is always one.

INTRODUCTION

The idea of presenting the influences of alchemy in a work as Romantic as *Heinrich von Ofterdingen* arose from an intuition during an investigation into the alchemical path of Goethe's faustian prototype, *Urfaust*. The faustian work, *Faust I* and *Faust II*, had already warranted an extensive study of hermetic philosophy in its composition. Broadly speaking, Agnes Bartscherer (1911) undertook this analysis in the first *Faust*; Carl Jung (1944) consistently used *Faust* as a case study for his investigations into alchemy and psychology; Ronald Gray (1952) traced Goethe's journey, reflecting his interest in alchemy; Alice Raphael (1964) focused on the second *Faust*; and Yvette Centeno's book (1978), the first Portuguese academic work on the subject, holds great value as it integrates previous studies and initiates a recovery of alchemy for literary, artistic, and philosophical studies. Numerous other studies could also be mentioned. Initially, my intent was to delve into the study of alchemy from the earliest faustian drafts, attempting to understand the evolution of Goethe's project over the decades he devoted to it.

During this investigation, being part of a comparative studies programme, I was interested in comparing this preliminary *Faust* with another unfinished work also influenced by hermetic philosophy. Under the guidance of Professor Claudia J. Fischer, I read Novalis's work and became aware of the author's interest in alchemy. However, *Heinrich von Ofterdingen* does not depict alchemical practice as Faust conducts it, whose father as well as he are practitioners of this laboratory art. The character Heinrich is an aspiring poet, and his journey begi ns to resemble ancient initiations related to various hermetic traditions. In any case, a brief passage in Alexandra Lembert's book *The Heritage of Hermes* promised a fruitful comparative study, stating that "Novalis and Goethe were not only theoretically interested in alchemy but are known to carry out (al)chemical experiments" (2004: 59).

Although several authors attest to the handling of hermetic references in Novalis's work, there is no project dedicated to reading *Heinrich von Ofterdingen* through the lens of alchemical thought. This may be because alchemy's role is not found in the action itself but in the way the novel is constructed and how imagination is employed. We believe this study can initiate a mature, systematic, and comprehensive reading of an alchemical movement that influences the characters' actions and provides insights into the world of alchemy. This initial project aims to recover and expand upon these considerations based on new insights and research developments.

We will begin by briefly presenting Novalis's setting, examining how the Romantic movement, Fichte's idealist philosophy, the Pietist religious movement, and other influences on his thought can be related to the alchemical context. Rather than a deep theoretical exploration of these lines of thought, we aim to show that these fields share commonalities that contributed to the lack of special attention given to alchemy, often overshadowed by romantic, idealist, and Pietist motivations in Novalis's work.

Next, it is crucial to trace the mystical, alchemical, and hermetic references in Novalis's intellectual journey. Although a reading of a work does not necessarily have to coincide with the author's referential world, but rather the reader's, it will be interesting to highlight what Novalis might have known about alchemy, considering that the symbol of Romanticism, the blue flower, created by Novalis, is deeply rooted in hermetic philosophy. We will discuss Novalis's metaphorical language, which implies a level of initiation into love and knowledge also found in alchemy. Jacob Böhme's thought will be a significant support for Novalis's ideas concerning alchemy, Gnosticism, and Kabbalah. We will examine some of Böhme's ideas, such as the figure of Sophia in Gnostic and Kabbalistic traditions, the seven powers of God, and the image of the hermaphrodite. We will also indicate Novalis's contacts with alchemical practice and theory and how they can be articulated with the

12

philosophical and religious lines previously outlined in the reading of *Ofterdingen*. This first part will conclude with the development of the image of the blue flower within the alchemical framework.

To avoid confusion and redundant explanations of alchemical notions, we have opted not to include a separate chapter solely on alchemical principles. We believe that the ideas developed in the first part can already provide a foundation for the alchemical aspects we wish to address. The reading of *Ofterdingen* will always be accompanied by necessary clarifications about alchemy relevant to this study. While it is impossible to cover everything about alchemy in this formal exercise, we sketch the main points that intersect with the ideas established in the first part.

Finally, we will read *Ofterdingen* from hermetic assumptions, demonstrating how the alchemical world is multifaceted, versatile, and fertile for literature. We do not argue that alchemy is the only or even the primary key to reading the work. However, we assert that its operations should be considered when examining Novalis's work and, ultimately, that there is a need to recover and update its significance within the philosophy of knowledge and cultural, literary, and artistic studies.

1

AN INCURABLE ROMANTIC

> Romantic poetry is a progressive
> universal poetry. Its purpose is not
> merely to reunite all the separate genres
> of poetry and bring poetry into contact
> with philosophy and rhetoric. It also
> aims to mix and merge poetry and prose,
> genius and criticism, artistic poetry and
> natural poetry, making poetry lively and
> sociable, and making life and society
> poetic.[1]
>
> (Friedrich Schlegel, *Athenaeum*, Fragment 116, 1798)

1.1 SOME IDEALISTIC LINES AND CHALLENGES

In 1798, Friedrich von Hardenberg published for the first time in the
Athenaeum, the journal of the Romantic movement founded by the
Schlegel brothers, adopting the name by which he would become best
known: Novalis. Novalis immediately aligned himself with
Romanticism through his friendship with Friedrich Schlegel. Initially,

---

[1] "Die romantische Poesie ist eine progressive Universalpoesie. Ihre
Bestimmung ist nicht bloß, alle getrennten Gattungen der Poesie wieder zu
vereinigen und die Poesie mit der Philosophie und Rhetorik in Berührung zu
setzen. Sie will und soll auch Poesie und Prosa, Genialität und Kritik,
Kunstpoesie und Naturpoesie bald mischen, bald verschmelzen, die Poesie
lebendig und gesellig und das Leben und die Gesellschaft poetisch machen."
All translations of quotations are by the author, unless otherwise indicated.

the terms "Romanticism" and "Romantic" were used pejoratively by those who disapproved of the idiosyncrasies of this new literary movement emerging from the ideas of these authors. There was not even an establishment of the so-called *romantische Schule*, as recorded in history. The concept "Romantic" appeared, primarily, in opposition to "Classical", as Gerhard Schulz notes (2004: 28). For example, if the classical referred to the art and culture of antiquity, the romantic tended to draw its imagery from the Middle Ages, in described landscapes and chivalric motifs, generally signifying "the tradition of Christian culture from the Middle Ages to the present day" (29). This motif would be extensively utilized in *Heinrich von Ofterdingen*, as we will observe.

Richard Littlejohns challenges the idea of Romanticism as a movement driven by wild imagination and frenetic inspiration. He points out that F. Schlegel and Novalis believed "inspiration has to be contained and even negated by the contrary impulse of rationality, by self-awareness and self-regulation" (61). This view is echoed in *Heinrich von Ofterdingen*, where the poet Klingsohr advises Heinrich that "enthusiasm without understanding is useless and dangerous" (1945: 250).[2] Such perspectives might complicate the perceived dichotomy between Romanticism and the Enlightenment. It is possible that the stark differences led to the creation of a stereotype, despite individual exemplary cases, without an actual profound opposition. The emphasis on "self-expression", as Littlejohns also notes, could indeed be both significant and contentious (2004: 62).

One of the activities of Romanticism, the *Symphilosophieren*, the act of philosophizing in a group, evokes a form of thought of the time, German Idealism, as Dennis Mahoney recalls (2004: 3). It was present in Novalis's philosophy, likely due to F. Schlegel's in-depth study of Johann Gottlieb Fichte's Idealism, later also studied by Novalis, both being well-versed in the premises of Kantian Idealism. Thus, Schlegel's idea was to counter the limited horizon concerning art and life of individual thoughts, emphasizing the importance of debate with others (3). This association between Romanticism and Idealism can help

---

[2] "Begeisterung ohne Verstand ist unnütz und gefährlich".

disassociate the Romantics from the image of "dreamy, moonstruck poets who relied on their emotions to create their art" (4). The valorization of imagination and the dream dimension is tied to profound conceptions of the self and the world in their philosophical, religious, and mystical aspects.

The Idealism begun by Kant, transcendental Idealism, revolutionizes Empiricism, which prevailed at the time, constructing something that could relate the inductive, empiricist method (where sensory perception is dominant) and the deductive method (broadly speaking, apprehension through the intellect). As Littlejohns observes, "Kant's achievement was to show that rationality could not produce absolute knowledge, functioning as it does through the limiting medium of subjective perception, so that it could serve only to analyze empirical phenomena" (65). The idealistic radicalization occurs with Fichte, expanding Kantian thought to its limits. As Littlejohns summarizes, Fichte concludes that "if all perceptions of reality are conditioned by our consciousness, [...] then in a sense we determine that reality; everything outside the ego is only the postulate of the ego, it is 'Nicht-Ich', non-ego" (65). Thus, without abandoning the primacy of reason, the notion that reality is conditioned by consciousness is allied with the deepening of imagination, for if reality is of consciousness, imagination can transmute it and create other forms of the real. *Ofterdingen* is a paradigm of this postulate. Until the end of the story, the reader witnesses a radically different world, in which imagination, knowledge, and poetry are the transmuters of reality.

Thus, poetic creation shifts away from Aristotle's mimetic principle, which is rooted in imitating the natural world, to embrace the "creation of new worlds through poetic experiment and imagination" (8). This evolution in Romantic *poiesis* is notably influenced by Fichtean Idealism, which posits that the self of humanity and the self of nature are fundamentally the same and strive for unity. This concept is crucial for Novalis, evident throughout his works, and serving as a central theme in *Heinrich von Ofterdingen*. As Novalis articulates in his *Fichte-Studien* (1795-6), "the highest principle must be, without exception, nothing given, but something freely made, something invented, something thought, in order to establish a general metaphysical system that begins with freedom and leads to freedom" (1960: 273).[3] For him, the act of creating freely, or "poetizing" (*erdichten*), was only achievable through the liberation of the imagination.

The interplay between idealistic thought and Novalis's literary contributions has proven influential for twentieth-century philosophy. Gaston Bachelard, for instance, aligns with Novalis by viewing imagination not as a mere imitation of reality or dependent on the senses—particularly sight—but as a dynamic process in itself. In *La psychanalyse du feu*, Bachelard delves into the Novalis complex, which is anchored in the concept of primordial fire generated by friction and the drive to explore the depths of objects to uncover a profound inner warmth. He illustrates his ideas with references from *Heinrich von Ofterdingen*: the spark ignited between Freya and Eros's sword or the exploration of mines, caves, and mountains where warmth emanates (1986: 69-70). For Novalis, imagination operates as a powerful force, much like fire and love, blending and intensifying through friction and shock as sources of both high and brief tension.

Novalis aligns seamlessly with Bachelard's portrayal in *Fragments d'une Poétique du feu*: "the philosopher pursues the absolute. He is wary of images, he does not need images. Ideas alone are sufficient for him" (1988: 11).[4] It is this inner dynamic, this movement of ideas, that empowers all worldly actions. By casting aside images and focusing exclusively on ideas, Novalis distances himself from rationalist approaches and emphasizes the act of creation—echoing the very essence of poetry, *poiein*. Bachelard also notes, "it is the experience of the fire of love that forms the basis of objective induction" (1986: 60).[5] This elemental fire of love sparks the unfolding of Heinrich's journey and intertwines with both poetry and alchemy. If ideas alone are

---

[3] "Das oberste Prinzip muß schlechterdings Nichts Gegebenes, sondern ein Frey Gemachtes, ein Erdichtetes, Erdachtes seyn, um ein allgemeines metaphysisches System zu begründen, das von Freyheit anfängt und zu Freyheit geht".

[4] "Le philosophe court à l'absolu. Il se méfie des images, il n'a pas besoin des images. Les idées lui suffisent".

[5] "C'est l'expérience du feu de l'amour qui est la base de l'induction objective".

sufficient, then the absolute becomes something achievable in concept, even if it remains perpetually out of reach. As Eustaquio Barjau encapsulates in the introduction to the Spanish edition of *Hymnen an die Nacht*, Novalis, the poet-philosopher, seeks "the ascent of the Universe to God; the reaction against the Enlightenment of his time, the confrontation of Night-Light, reason-feeling: through night and feeling, man can access everything, the Beyond, the Absolute" (1982: 1).[6] The absolute thus emerges as a synthesis of opposites, mirroring the core principles of alchemy.

In this way, the concept of the absolute becomes more coherent through the integration of reason and imagination, if only potentially: "thought contains the potential for development, for self-transcendence, even self-contradiction, or at least contains a built-in awareness of its own incompleteness, in other words that it is capable of self-ironizing" (Littlejohns 2004: 67). Novalis finds a central challenge in Fichte's theory of knowledge: how can we know something about being if only being is? This "being" refers to all the activity of consciousness, which Fichte sees as self-sufficiency. Being would be absolute action, in which the agent and object of action are identified. However, Novalis realizes that, in affirming this identity, we are already dividing being. That is, by reflecting on being, we break its unity, as if there were knowledge about being; as if being and what being knows about itself were separated. In sum, the objectification of being makes it inoperable in its essence.

Novalis then proposes that the consciousness of being is only its being-there, its presence. In other words, it is its image. Being is closed off within itself, yet its existence manifests as a phenomenalization, becoming an image in thought. This is not merely a reflection but an active creation of the image: existence is an imagination crafted by the being itself; it is the means by which the being preserves itself through created images. However, access to the purity of being is never achieved because these images, from the perspective of being as it is,

---

[6] "La ascensión del Universo a Dios; la reacción antiilustrada de su tiempo, el enfrentamiento Noche-Luz, razón-sentimiento: a través de la noche y del sentimiento el hombre puede acceder a todo, al Más Allá, al Absoluto".

cannot be anything but mere presence. As we read in *Philosophische Studien*, in the section "Über das Bewusstsein", "On Consciousness":

> What sort of relationship is knowledge? It is a being outside of being, yet it is in being. (Dividing - uniting.) Consciousness is a being outside of being in being. But what is that? The outside of being does not have to be true being. An incorrect being outside of being is an image. - Therefore, what is outside of being must be an image of being in being. Consciousness is consequently an image of being in being. (1945b: 151)[7]

Thus, for Novalis, the image will always belong to the realm of appearance; it is, in essence, the appearance of being, a creation. Existence is therefore fiction, but fiction of its own fiction, leading us to conclude that the absolute is never truly known; rather, its identity is only understood through the liberation of imaginative forces, which create a synthesis of sensory experience. As an image of the image, existence becomes primordial chaos, in a hyperstimulation of the absolute, which reveals itself in its finite appearances: the awareness that truth is the appearance of truth. The Fichtean image preserves the being that is placed into image, while the Novalisian perspective begins with the chaotic and confused: is it the image that conceives the absolute, or does the absolute dramatically enter common existence? Is the word the performative appearance of the grasping of what is found in this chaos, in primordial night?

1.2. PIETISM: FAITH AND THE VALUE OF THE SELF

Glauben und Liebe oder Der König und die Königin (*Faith and Love or The King and the Queen*), the first work to come to light, presents a

---

[7] "Was fur eine Beziehung ist das Wissen? Es ist ein Sein außer dem Sein, das doch im Sein ist. (Teilen - vereinen.) Das Bewusstsein ist ein Sein außer dem Sein im Sein. Was ist aber das? Das außer dem Sein muss kein rechtes Sein sein. Ein unrechtes Sein außer dem Sein ist ein Bild. - Also muss jenes außer dem Sein ein Bild des Seins im Sein sein. Das Bewusstsein ist folglich ein Bild des Seins im Sein".

collection of fragments that metaphorically construct its ideal of humanity. This ideal is associated with the monarchical ideal, symbolized by the king and queen, representing an education and a state of perfection to be aspired to by humankind: "the educational means to this distant goal is a king"(1945b: 55).[8] Novalis, who seeks not only aesthetic transformation but also a form of social interaction grounded in intersubjectivity, explores an attempt to balance the absolute freedom of the subject with hierarchically ordered structures. He proposes a dynamic relationship between symbol and representation (Panno, 2005: 57-58). Through his work, Novalis suggests an approach in which form and order emerge from continuous interaction and exchange among individuals.

Despite the significant impact Novalis's ideas garnered between 1805 and 1810 from Romanticism and Restoration Catholicism, he remained relatively uninvolved in political matters (60). His stance was more reserved and participatory within the early Romantic circles and philosophical circuits of Dresden and Jena. For instance, Novalis was interested in the concept of corporations, particularly in the context of a "microcosmic emergence of an artistic composition of man" (60). Essentially, the focus is on the relationship between the individual and the state through an aestheticization of the world via transcendental action. In this sense, Novalis aims for an inner revolution that enables a truly transformative social and political change: self-recognition occurs through interaction with the other.

The transcendental self of the subject is symbolized by the king, a unifying and restorative symbol of humanity, a vital principle of the state, akin to the sun, by which all live in fullness. Novalis does not advocate an exclusively monarchical form of governance with coercive authority. Instead, his intention is to create a movement of coincidence between the king and the citizen, between the one and the many, the microcosm and the macrocosm, metaphorically speaking. The state is understood as an organism, whose will guides and harmonizes all challenges of human life, leading all citizens to a state of reflection and reciprocity. Thus, the king and queen serve as metaphors that embody

[8] "Das Erziehungsmittel zu diesem fernen Ziel ist ein König".

the spiritual relationship imagined by cosmic hierogamy, so dear to alchemy, as a sacred union of opposites from which something more perfect will emerge; as we will also see in *Ofterdingen*.

Therefore, if the king and queen represent a mythological pair, a model for all citizens, then the state will serve to repeat the ritual of correspondence between microcosm and macrocosm, between the human and the world. The ultimate function will be the continuous act of transforming the subject into a future king. The valorization of the self, encouraged by the quest for identity, may have contributed to the growing influence of the Pietist movement of that time, even though it originated in the fifteenth/sixteenth centuries, and vice versa. Broadly speaking, this religious movement emphasizes the predominance of individual experiences of each believer in interpreting the Scriptures and in contact with the divine, moving away from Lutheran orthodoxy and implementing personal and congregational freedom, which disregards ecclesiastical organizations.

Pietism energizes the idea of a Christian community and a monarchy where each citizen could be a king. Novalis philosophically and poetically develops under the influence of this religious movement and,[9] for this reason, will always be severely criticized by Goethe, as noted by Hans-Joachim Mähl in his essay, "Goethes Urteil über Novalis: Ein Beitrag zur Geschichte der Kritik an der deutschen Romantik" (1967: 130–270). In a letter to poet and friend Johann Peter Eckermann dated April 2, 1829, Goethe asserts: "I call the Classical the healthy and the Romantic the sick" (2013: 393).[10] This aphoristic synthesis may imply more than just a condemnation of Romanticism. The sickness of Romanticism could indeed be focused, beyond Catholicism, on Pietism. David Hill defines it as a bipolar movement: while it views life through religious meanings, secularizing Protestantism and removing power from the church, it also attributes to "everyday experiences the intensity and the transcendental meaningfulness that had previously been the province of religion, and thus they fueled a new intensity of the inner life

---

[9] Other romantics later converted to Catholicism, such as F. Schlegel and Clemens Brentano.

[10] "Das Klassische nenne ich das Gesunde und das Romantische das Kranke".

in literature" (2003: 6). Both Goethe and Novalis, along with their contemporaries, received an education heavily influenced by this movement, whose practice of extreme sentimentalism was vehemently criticized by Goethe, as demonstrated in the edition organized by Georg Wittkowski in *Verlorene Klassik? Ein Symposium* (1986: 52-73). Notably, Goethe experienced intense faith and maintained contact with friends and family who were thoroughly Pietist as late as 1768, as noted by Hill (2003: 9).

Indeed, "Goethe's adamant rejection of enthusiastic tendencies (*Schwärmerei*) was a fundamental component of his Enlightenment worldview", as asserted by Arnd Bohm (2004: 41), who discusses Goethe's "intense ire" (41) toward Catholicism and any mysticism, which he viewed as "irrational thought" (41). Bohm attributes this aversion as one of the reasons Goethe rejected Romanticism, citing the poet's sarcastic characterization: "the neo-Catholic sentimentalism [...] the monastery-brotherish, star-baldish monstrosity" (41).[11] However, while Bohm interprets this tone as a general critique, Johannes Weber, in *Goethe und die Jungen*, shows that it specifically targets one of the proselytizing writings of the Riepenhausen brothers. Recently converted to Catholicism, their work displayed religious fervour and an intention to convert their readers. It also served as a mocking attack on Wilhelm Wackenroder's essay "Herzensergießungen eines kunstliebenden Klosterbruders" and Ludwig Tieck's work "Franz Sternbalds Wanderungen", as demonstrated by Weber (2013: 50). Weber illustrates Goethe's disdain for newly converted Christians, his displeasure with impulsive sentimentality,[12] and his rejection of excessive mystical enthusiasm and uncontrolled imagination in Romantic works. Regarding his beliefs, Goethe confides to Johann Caspar Lavater in a letter of 1782

---

[11] "Die neukatholische Sentimentalität [...] das klosterbruderisirende, sternbaldisirende Unwesen".

[12] Despite this opinion, *Werther* contains another type of intense sentimentalism, imposed by *Empfindsamkeit*, another German cultural movement characterized by sentimentalism, competing with Romanticism. Therefore, it is worth noting that in the long life and multiple interests of Goethe, his ideas may have changed over time and with experiences.

that he is decidedly non-Christian (1901: 209). Goethe might have condemned fervent sentimentalism stemming from exacerbated religiosity as exposed in literary production, yet he did not necessarily oppose a holistic knowledge that also includes the study of mystical areas, valid for the study of nature and thought.[13]

On the one hand, familial education is nourished by religion, and intellectual education is manifested through scepticism and rationalism. On the other, Kant's limitation of empirical action and protagonism leaves room for belief in the transcendental and spiritual experience of the self. Broadly, personal experience, the freedom of imagination, focus on consciousness, and emancipation of self-expression, encapsulated in the Romantic project, intersect with historical, social, philosophical, and religious factors. Among other developments in Universal History, we highlight the ten years of the French Revolution; the subsequent fall of the monarchy; Robespierre's dictatorship and Napoleon's rise to power; these events disrupt the Holy Roman Empire, which, on account of its long history and geographic expanse, faced various fracturing problems, culminating in its dissolution in 1806. This instability challenges national identity and aligns with the Idealist interpretation of phenomenal reality as dependent on individual consciousness, despite the coexistence of heterogeneous approaches; primarily, among Kant, Fichte, Hegel, and Schelling. The subject's experience becomes central to the experience of the world.[14]

---

[13] Another factor that might have caused Goethe to clash with Romanticism, especially in its early stages, would be his age and experience, which led him to diverge from certain political and social views of younger authors. Mahoney discusses this difference: Goethe agrees with the need for political changes but does not support major modifications in social structures. On the other hand, the new generation embraced the more radical changes brought by the French Revolution, seeing them as progress, as they were teenagers or young adults. Cf. Mahoney (2004: 7). Indeed, in 1789, Goethe was already 40 years old, while Friedrich Schlegel and Novalis were 17.

[14] This awareness of a fragmented individual identity, exacerbated by the fragmentation of national identity, already concerned the members of *Sturm und Drang*. Cf. Hill (2003: 22).

These factors are present without advocating a system of causality. Schulz clarifies this point: nationalist ideas are not part of Romanticism's programme, even though they coincide with the resurgence of nationalist consciousness for the historical reasons mentioned above, and religious values, particularly Catholic, lose relevance with the Enlightenment and French Enlightenment. Authors like Novalis incorporate mystical thoughts in their works, often as a metaphorical resource (2004: 32). In summary, we emphasize early German Romanticism as "the literary attempts toward the end of the eighteenth and at the beginning of the nineteenth century that try to invoke a Christian-European consciousness and depart from the traditions of forms and the mainly mythological imagery of classical antiquity" (33). It is through this narrow path that we also understand the relevance of alchemy.

1.3 LOVE AND KNOWLEDGE: THE SECRET LANGUAGE OF ALCHEMY

In the introduction to Novalis's *Glauben und Liebe*, we read:

> When one wants to speak secretly with a few people in a large, mixed society and one is not sitting next to them, one must speak in a special language. This special language can either be a foreign language according to tone or according to images. The latter will be a language of tropes and riddles. [...] Every true secret must of itself exclude the profane. Whoever understands it is, by virtue, and rightfully, initiated. The mystical expression is more of a mental stimulus. All truth is ancient. The appeal of novelty lies only in variations of expression. [...] What one loves, one finds everywhere and sees similarities everywhere. The greater the love, the broader and more varied this similar world. My beloved is the abbreviation of the universe, the universe is the elongation of my beloved. (1945b: 49-50)[15]

---

[15] "Wenn man mit Wenigen in einer großen, gemischten Gesellschaft etwas Heimliches reden will und man sitzt nicht nebeneinander, so muss man in

Secret and special languages appear in various traditions. The metaphorical and allegorical treatment of language is a hallmark of mystical writings, resistance to censorship, and the desire to recreate language. Orphic and Platonic traditions tell us that "many carry the thyrsus — say those initiated into the Mysteries — but few are the true enthusiasts" (Plato, *Phaedrus*, 69c). Similarly, we find this right of the initiated to access truth in Matthew 22:14: "many are called, but few are chosen". The true enthusiasts, etymologically those who have the god within them, would be the true philosophers. Etymologically, the profane is one who stands outside the temple.

Thus, Novalis calls for a non-literal reading of his writings, suggesting that he is an enthusiast who writes in a special and secret language that only other enthusiasts, within the temple, with the god within them, in love with knowledge, can understand. The enthusiast, the philosopher, the chosen one, who carries the secret and special language, possesses an extreme love for knowledge, truth, and self. According to Novalis, those who love find similarities of what they love everywhere. The ability to metaphorize, to find similarities in the Aristotelian sense, is the ability to love, to know everything, and to recover the unity of everything. Thus, as will be shown in *Heinrich von Ofterdingen*, the poet has the responsibility to improve the world through love, uniting all dissonances. Through love, the microcosm and macrocosm recognize and correspond with each other. In *Ofterdingen*, the importance of the force of love is constantly reiterated, as this force is responsible for a reconciliation between the self and the other, between the subjective and the objective.

einer besondern Sprache reden. Diese besondre Sprache kann entweder eine Ton nach oder den Bildern nach fremde Sprache sein. Dies letztere wird eine Tropen und Rätselsprache sein. [...] Jedes wahre Geheimnis muss die Profanen von selbst ausschließen. Wer es versteht, ist von selbst, mit Recht, Eingeweihter. Der mystische Ausdruck ist ein Gedankenreiz mehr. Alle Wahrheit ist uralt. Der Reiz der Neuheit liegt nur in den Variationen des Ausdrucks. [...] Was man liebt, findet man überall und sieht überall Ähnlichkeiten. Je großer die Liebe, desto weiter und mannigfaltiger diese ähnliche Welt. Meine Geliebte ist die Abbreviatur des Universums, das Universum die Elongatur meiner Geliebten".

The correspondence between the beloved and the universe and her presence in everything in the world, as exposed by Novalis in the previous passage, are Gnostic and Kabbalistic marks that will be evident in our reading of *Ofterdingen*. Alchemy shares the same interest in concealing its truths from the outset of its written records. The alchemist Nicolas Flamel, in his *Le bréviaire*, warns his nephew, to whom he dedicates his hermetic writings, and consequently his readers:

> Thus, rightly understand and interpret the Sermons of the Philosophers on the Secret, but do not take their words literally, for they would not benefit you, as they are meant to be understood according to their nature. (2012: 5)[16]

Zosimos of Panopolis, in the third century CE, the first alchemist whose life and work can be more thoroughly traced, inaugurates metaphorical and allegorical writing in alchemy, as he himself notes, when he says:

> The woman without a husband does not conceive nor give birth, but when a man is with her who is not barren, she conceives and bears a child that resembles them both, so if the father is a king, his son is a king like him. And the hen, when she lays […] and incubates her eggs, and those eggs are from [the participation of] the male cock, his young hatch. But if those eggs are from earth […] and then she incubates them, nothing hatches from them. [...] this is a metaphor, so consider it and it will not be very difficult for you to comprehend. (Hallum 2008: 339-41)

In this passage, besides the confession of metaphorical writing, we also find the image of the king associated with conception. In any case, we will not delve into the full meaning of Zosimos's message here. It is

---

[16] "Suis donc de droit engin et entendement les Sermons des Philosophes écrivant du Secret, mais ne prends leurs dires comme disent, car ne te seraient profit, ainsi que veulent être entendus selon nature".

important to note that there is a necessity to recommend to the reader that he interpret the alchemical text metaphorically. Lawrence Principe notes that "Zosimos employs a technique that would become typical for alchemical authors: the use of Decknamen" (2013: 18), covering a name with another name to pass the message secretly. The function continues to be to communicate one's texts to others, not merely to obscure them. Thus, the choice of Decknamen is not arbitrary, for if it were, no one would be able to decode the writings. Secretism reduces the number of readers-decoders, but does not eliminate them. Still, only initiates and adepts can interpret the hermetic texts. Only they know the codes.

Metaphors and coded names become alchemical symbols that, from treatise to treatise, from alchemist to alchemist, gain some differences according to the experience, readings, beliefs and philosophies of their authors. Thus, the alchemical process can be narrated as a story in which the king and queen represent the sun and the moon, the male and the female, sulphur and mercury, who marry, copulate, give birth, kill eagles and dragons, die, resurrect, and, in each (con)text, can signify different stages of the alchemical work, featuring crows, swans, salamanders, phoenixes, etc.

However, the necessity of a special language also raises more practical underlying issues. One of the factors contributing to the secrecy to which alchemical texts, practices, and authors were subjected is the close relationship between alchemy and astrology, heavily censured from the first century CE (Lindsay 1970: 54). Another factor is that alchemists were grouped with blacksmiths, miners, metallurgists, and were all seen as forgers who made money, fake gold, or poor-quality gold. This prejudice was exacerbated in the second and third centuries CE by the economic crisis of the Roman Empire (54). Zosimos alerts to the need for a tradition kept secret to avoid persecution and accusations (59).

A text dated to the first or second century CE, *Physikà kai mystikà* by pseudo-Democritus, suggests in its title the necessity of secrecy. "Mystika", incorrectly translated for a long time as something "mystical", means something that must be kept secret. As Principe notes, "for pseudo-Democritus, these processes are mystika, that is, secret, because they are lucrative artisanal processes — trade secrets" (2013: 12). These texts show recipes similar to those in the Leiden and Stockholm papyri, the oldest and original alchemical texts found in Egypt, written in Greek, dated to the third century BCE, containing practical recipes related to crafts, goldsmithing, metallurgy, cosmetics, and textile dyeing, with tests to determine the purity of metals. It is plausible to consider that alchemical practice is older and that these texts are the result of an oral tradition (10-11). Nevertheless, due to these factors and others, recipes considered alchemical should be kept secret.

In any case, the coded language reinforces the importance of revelation in the act of reading by the initiate. This is a Gnostic and Kabbalistic mark in alchemy, relating to the idea of a loving relationship with knowledge and with the entire material world. This loving attraction between divine wisdom and the material world makes truth accessible to humans, and thus the need for it to be worked through language so it can be reached through revelation, that is, through the mature reading of both the creation process and the concealment process of what is written. This work is developed by Jacob Böhme, who revolutionizes Lutheranism, influencing Pietism with Paracelsian alchemy, as we will see.

As Mihai Stroe observes, Novalis was deeply interested in thinking about the male-female binary, the fusion between the masculine and the feminine, and for the researcher this is one of the main reasons that lead Novalis to alchemy and the conceptions of Paracelsus and Böhme (2007: 61-69). This interest revolutionizes alchemy itself, understanding that poetry and love would lead to the alchemical objectives of the perfection of the being. The alchemical work would, therefore, be realized in the union of the male-female pair. However, beyond the spiritual dimension, Novalis is also concerned with the aesthetic dimension of Romanticism, catalysed by love.

The eighteenth century is particularly rich in the intersection of lines of thought that bring together political, religious, mystical, philosophical, artistic and intellectual dimensions. Naturally, we find the young Novalis immersed in this constellation. However, it is not just about experiencing all these forms of life and perception of reality, but also how all these fields of action reflect upon one another. Therefore, it will always be difficult to separate what comes from the alchemical tradition, which by itself already condenses different forms of thought and becomes increasingly idiosyncratic, with each scholar and practitioner subjecting it to their own experience. It is, above all, Christianity that has shaped, up to the present day, alchemical conceptions.

The Christian tradition of the Middle Ages, a strong strand of the early Romantic imagination, represents on one hand a matrix for Hermetic philosophy, whose alchemical practice draws upon Christian characters, messages, and symbols from the Renaissance onwards. On the other hand, Christianity also appropriates the alchemical tradition, which had already been overlaid with various cultural and religious dynamics. Specifically, and briefly, alchemy encompasses pre-Socratic philosophy, with theories of the conjunction of opposites, the creation of the universe, the movement of being in becoming, the universal element, and the primacy of fire as the logos; Orphic and Pythagorean conceptions; the good-evil dichotomy of Zoroastrianism; Platonism, with Plato understood as "the founder of alchemy as a science" (Lindsay 1970: 14), particularly focusing on the notions of demiurge and creator-craftsman; Stoicism, broadly speaking, with the enhancement of the self; Gnosticism, in its struggle between spirit and matter; and Kabbalah, in the decoding of the hidden symbolism of the universe. We will thus see one of the most significant avenues of the development of alchemical interest in the eighteenth century, particularly in Novalis.

1.3.1. JACOB BÖHME AND THE PIETISTS

In the introduction to the 1832 publication *Die Geschichte der Alchemie* by historian Karl Christoph Schmieder, theologian Marco Frenschkowski comments that the legacies of the mystic Jacob Böhme and alchemical authors are well-present in pietist groups (2005: 17). Regarding the relationship between Pietism and alchemy, Gray suggests that it was the religious aspect, present since medieval alchemy, explored by Böhme and Gottfried Arnold, that led the pietist movement to integrate some alchemical concepts (2010: 4).

Pietism found a place in alchemy to incorporate the sacrificial example of Christ. As Gray recalls, alchemy was able to develop significantly through the combination of Greek philosophical tradition with Orphism (250), where the sacrifice of Orpheus evokes that of Dionysus and prefigures that of Christ, identifying him with the Philosopher's Stone; the fixed salt, as it is called (20). Furthermore, the researcher recounts the pietist-alchemical fervour, exemplified in Johann Hector von Klettenberg, for whom "the process of 'Nigredo', the descent into Hell, meant the complete renunciation of earthly pleasures, of love and dancing and fine clothes, and the annihilation of self-will" (252). As previously mentioned, Goethe, initially influenced by Klettenberg, distanced himself from this austere and radical stance, contrary to Novalis.

One of the ideas revived in Pietism is the chiliastic belief in the return of the golden age or paradise on earth, or the second coming of Christ for a thousand-year reign. In *Die Christenheit oder Europa*, Novalis promises: "just be patient; it will come, it must come, the holy time of eternal peace, when the new Jerusalem will be the capital of the world" (1946c: 34).[17] The title already indicates an identification between Christendom and Europe, as if to say: calling one or the other by the same name. This quest for unity, both individual and collective, spiritual and political, becomes apparent.

With Marsilio Ficino in the fifteenth century, Renaissance philosophy aimed to reintegrate Platonic thought and Hermetic texts, such as the *Corpus Hermeticum*, attributed to Hermes Trismegistus, the legendary patron of alchemy, to elevate magic and mysticism to more intellectual and scholarly circles and to carry out a reform of the Church. This latter intention was especially led by Giordano Bruno in the sixteenth century (Yates 1964: 20-235). The consolidation of alchemy within Christianity occurs primarily with the alchemist physician Paracelsus in the sixteenth century and his follower Jacob Böhme in the seventeenth century, a mystical German shoemaker and Lutheran, who renews alchemical thought, reinforcing Gnostic,

[17] "Nur Geduld, sie wird, sie muß kommen die heilige Zeit des ewigen Friedens, wo das neue Jerusalem die Hauptstadt der Welt seyn wird".

31

Kabbalistic, and Christian marks in alchemy.

Kabbalah, an esoteric school of thought in the tradition of Jewish mysticism, means in Hebrew "the received words" or "hidden wisdom" and constitutes the cornerstone of Jewish esoteric tradition. Understanding God and the mysteries of the universe, attempting to reconcile an unknowable God with a knowable one, a good God who is the creator of everything and infinite with his finite creation where evil resides, are its objectives. Gershom Scholem made a significant contribution to the relationship between Kabbalah, Gnosticism, and alchemy. One of the best-known texts, *Zohar*, first known in the thirteenth century, uses the transmutation of silver into gold as a metaphor for the transmutation of the soul, in a mystical interpretation of Gnostic origin, also speaking of the mystical gold (Scholem 2015: 38). The alchemist Cornelius Agrippa in the fifteenth century already involved Kabbalah with alchemy, even creating a deviation he called Kabbalistic alchemy, which combined experimental practices of a magical and ritualistic nature (92-4). As the seventeenth-century alchemist Heinrich Khunrath states, "Kabbalah, magic, and alchemy must be united and must be practised together" (in Scholem 2015: 97).[18]

Gnosticism encompasses various religious movements, more relevant in the second and third centuries CE, where salvation was attained through revealed knowledge. This revelation would bring awareness of the divine origin of the human being. This knowledge, as Principe notes, is the key to freeing the body from passions and the material world (2013: 20). Gnostic dualism, unlike Zoroastrianism, centres the struggle between good and evil in the opposition of spirit and matter, taking on pessimistic contours, as the soul is imprisoned in the body; an idea already thought with Orphism in the fifth century BCE, as highlighted by Ralf Liedtke (1996: 49). The Socratic idea of *soma-sema*, which makes the body a prison for the soul, attempts to be overcome in alchemy by affirming life, by the creative impulse that seeks to alter the course of nature in life itself. As Alexander Roob observes, the Platonic demiurge transforms in Gnosticism into a

---

[18] "Kabbalah, magia e alchimia devono essere unite e unite devono essere praticate".

creator of an imperfect and corrupt work, requiring the intervention of the alchemist to perfect it (2006: 19).

The main connection between Gnosticism, Kabbalah, and alchemy is the figure of Sophia. As Scholem notes, the Gnostics call her the "daughter of light" and, in Kabbalah, she is related to the Shekinah, the dwelling place of God (Scholem 2001: 82). Sophia is the holder of wisdom, and God dwells in her. She is the divine soul and the creative force of the material world: "The "paths of Sophia" are therefore fundamental forces that emanate from her or in which she manifests herself. They are [...] the instruments of creation" (22).[19] The Sophia of the Gnostics is also seen as the Tree of Sephiroth or Tree of Life of the Kabbalists (70), divided into ten interconnected parts, forming the emanations of God. However, Sophia has a dual nature. She is this higher Sophia but also has a lower counterpart.

In Zosimus's treatises, the path of knowledge through revelation is already indicated; an inner work granted by God (Hallum 2008: 337). It is also explained that metal is formed of two parts: a body and a spirit, the latter being responsible for the metal's colour and identity (Principe 2013: 16). Thus, the metallurgical metaphor of alchemy is created: the sophic soul of love and wisdom, rooted in the body, which needed to be extracted to be revealed. Zosimus reinterprets the original man, Adam, as a being imprisoned to be saved by Christ, the master educator of matter, who would have taught humans to reject their harmful bodies (21).

Sophia represents the movement of revelation, thus a dual movement of concealment and unveiling. The Gnostic-Kabbalistic myth narrates Sophia's fall, being attracted by the primordial formless mass. From this conjunction, humanity is born, whose corrupt matter imprisons Sophia (80), thus justifying the existence of a divine spark in humans. The first being, primordial Adam or Adam Kadmon, was androgynous. However, he loses his unity, separating from his celestial wife Sophia. The destiny of this being involves seeking completeness, living with a vulnerable and sick body, in need. His relationship and

---

[19] "Die 'Wege der Sophia' sind also Grundkräfte, die von ihr ausgehen oder in denen sie sich darstellt. Sie sind [...] die Instrumente der Schöpfung".

identification with the world become irreconcilable, marked by debt and guilt (Roob 2006: 149). This establishes the origin of our imperfection and the need to find, through wisdom and love, gold, perfection, Sophia, the return to the celestial origin or matrix.

Paracelsus revolutionizes alchemy, taking the medieval system to modern chemistry, conceiving new processes. Alchemy, for him, is the art of finishing subtle nature, which does not want to be realized but instead provides the tools to be perfected by humans (Paracelsus 2008: 210). Humans would thus be destined to know and enhance all of nature by knowing how to handle the elements of the world. According to the alchemist, the transmutation caused by fire teaches that life is a combustion, that the body is wood, and living is letting it burn (318). Sophia, the soul imprisoned in the human body, becomes for Paracelsus the light of nature, an eternal light synonymous with the Holy Spirit (19). Chaos, the primordial mass, constitutes the universal seed of the material world, containing in itself the substances mercury, sulphur, salt; respectively, soul, spirit, and body (410). Chaos is the air, containing heaven and earth, an egg where life and essence reside (170). These and other notions will prove important for Böhme and, consequently, for the early Romantics.

In *Aurora oder die Morgenröte im Aufgang* (1612), Böhme presents the seven qualities/forces/spirits of God, which also exist in every micro-organism, depicted as a wheel or a sphere. Böhme divides these into two groups: the first three relate to the earth and the other four belong to the heavens.

The first quality is the wrath [*der Zorn*] of God and the second is the love [*die Liebe*] of God, which Böhme calls celestial Sophia or the bride of God (2013: 270-80), with the former being masculine and the latter feminine. The first is described as an eternal abyss, chaos, primordial uncreated will, termed as the nothing [*das Nichts*] or the uncreated [*der Ungrund*]. It represents the world before creation. The second is a force that expands in time and space, in opposition to the first, termed as the something [*das Etwas*] (796-7). The "nothing" and the "something" struggle, like darkness and light, to create the world. Moving in opposite directions, they cause the wheel to turn, explaining the movement of the planets (778).

This rotation is a third force, the offspring of the first two (236), which equates to the Philosopher's Stone. However, the Stone is not the third element but the product of the three elements combined, making it a fourth entity and simultaneously a single thing, reminiscent of the equation by the alchemist Maria the Prophetess: "one becomes two, and two become three, and through the third, the fourth accomplishes unity; thus two are no longer one" (Berthelot 1888: 389).[20] As Ronald Gray reflects, "the third Quality thus corresponds to the alchemical return to the first matter and to the mother" (2010: 42). Therefore, the three qualities represent the Holy Trinity and, alchemically, salt, mercury, and sulphur.

The other four relate to the celestial sphere [*Astra*]. The fourth force is the transition from the third to the fifth (Böhme 2013: 290), akin to a death leading to rebirth. The fourth force facilitates this process, which Böhme defines as heat born in the waters, the true source of life (452). The fifth, sixth, and seventh are analogous to the terrestrial ones but apply to the higher sphere. The fifth represents rebirth; the sixth is a higher form of love (316), akin to a Platonic path. Gray, alongside researcher Howard Brinton, suggests that if the second force is earthly love, more visually orientated, the sixth is linked to the auditory sense, as an "intelligible sound" (Gray: 2010: 45). The term Böhme uses is "*der Schall*" [sound, resonance, echo], which he claims is related to Mercury (2013: 284). The seventh quality is also correlated with the Philosopher's Stone, as the third force was, both being seeds. It is the conjunction of all six, representing nature itself (470).

In summary, Böhme calls the process involving these forces wisdom. For Kabbalists, wisdom is represented by a virgin, which for Böhme is Sophia or Aurora and can correspond to the Philosopher's Stone and the hermaphrodite, being both masculine and feminine. Wisdom is the conjunction of opposites. Gray further asserts that the union of the earthly ternary group with the celestial quaternary group represents the marriage of earth and heaven (2010: 45), aligning with Paracelsus's concept of the egg containing earth and heaven.

---

[20] "Un devient deux, et deux deviennent trois, et au moyen du troisième, le quatrième accomplit l'unité; ainsi deux ne font plus qu'un".

Another concept expanded by Böhme and developed by Novalis is that of the androgynous or hermaphroditic hermetic figure. In hermetic thought, there is the image of a superior being that fuses masculine and feminine qualities. The true mage contained the synthesis of dualities. Over time, the mage is no longer just a man but an inclusive image, achievable by any gender. The androgynous figure symbolizes divine power and esoteric knowledge:

> the symbol of the androgyne, which goes back to the earliest mythic conceptions of the divinity, represents the all-inclusive character of the Godhead that contains within itself all the conflicting and contrasting properties of existence, including the most fundamental differentiation of all between the two sexes. (Walsh 1983: 20)

In this sense, for Böhme, true human nature is divine, hence androgynous. The alchemical marriage symbolizes the reconciliation of fixed and volatile elements, reason and imagination, reality and perception, and, particularly from Böhme's perspective, signifies power and divinity: the immaculate conception of Mary and the extraction of Eve from Adam's body are the most well-known examples.

By conceiving Sophia as the wisdom of God, accessible to humans, Böhme establishes a connection between the image of the hermetic androgyne and the figure of Sophia. The marriage between the human and God's wisdom signifies a return to a pure state before the fall of Adam. The wheel of God's seven qualities, as described by Böhme, represents a process of uniting humanity with divinity. Sophia, Adam's first woman, must reconcile with humanity to achieve the most sublime state of completeness. Naturally, this process could only be developed on an aesthetic plane:

> the doctrine of androgyny has not simply an ethical meaning; it also holds significance for poetry and art. The highest beauty must be androgynous [...]. But if the masculine or feminine form is to be beautiful in the highest sense of the term, it must rise above the sexual contrast and express a combination of the nature of man and woman. (Martensen 1885: 248)

We will see how Novalis attempts aesthetically to revive the image of the androgyne in *Ofterdingen*, making it paradigmatic in Romantic aesthetics.

1.3.2. NOVALIS AND THE ALCHEMICAL MEANDERS

Mihai Stroe notes that Romanticism follows the patterns of the alchemical process: working from chaos, transforming and organizing this chaos, synthesizing dualities, and, above all, the possibility of spiritual perfectibility, operating on the corrupted matter that is human matter, to achieve perfection, redemption, and revelation (2007: 71-73). Naturally, as we have already seen, this derives from the Gnostics and Pietists.

However, we must disagree with Stroe on one small observation: the author tells us that, unlike alchemy, Romanticism never reaches its final stage in the process of creating a perfect unity (73). On the one hand, alchemy never achieved this. It is something projected and dreamed of. Flamel claims to have succeeded, for example, as we read in his *Le Bréviaire*. However, we surely know that he did not. On the other hand, we also cannot assert that alchemy and Romanticism did not reach their final stages. We can, however, question what those final stages are. It seems to us that, more than arriving at the perfect unity of all opposites, the intention might have been to create an impossible goal—the state of divinity—so that the process would always be infinite, favouring its continuity and incompleteness. In other words, focusing on error and experience, on the process of infinite and ever-open knowledge, on the constant mutation and improvement of matter—these may be the great successes achieved by both alchemy and Romanticism.

As Joachim Mähl points out in his study *Die Idee des goldenen Zeitalters im Werk des Novalis*, the search for restructuring develops in the thought of an ideal earthly monarchy (1994: 245), anchored in eighteenth-century Pietism, as observed. In *Heinrich von Ofterdingen*, as I will demonstrate, the symbol of the Holy Sepulchre is invoked, in the desire for a temporal and spatial zone identical to the golden age, the homeland: *immer nach Hause* [always home] is the eternal message of the blue flower, soon to be studied. Historian Alexei Pimenov comments that, for Novalis, the childhood of humanity, towards which one should strive, was in India. At Novalis's time, Sanskrit gained particular interest due to the discovery of the Indo-European origin of languages. Returning to the homeland would, therefore, be to India, as a "metaphysical entity by which the poet's soul seeks to be absorbed" (Pimenov 2020: 61). Indeed, Novalis wrote in the notes to *Ofterdingen* that "the feminine Orient / the oriental motherland is also poetry" (1945: 331).[21] Thus, the cradle of humanity is also poetry.

Therefore, the return to the oriental, poetic origin and, in the religious aspect, before the fall of humanity, is inscribed in the Romantic commitment as a way of return. Thus, Novalis states in *Fragmente des Jahres 1798*: "the world must be romanticized. In this way, one finds the original meaning again" (1945: 38).[22] This mission is also announced by Friedrich Schlegel, in the progressive universal poetry, cited in the epigraph to our introduction. For these Romantics, poetry has this transcendental effect, where nature itself does not transform but reveals itself as romantic. To reveal oneself as romantic is to return to its original enchantment. F. Schlegel writes in *Athenäeum*, "Poesie der Poesie" (1960: 241) [poetry of poetry], in a self-reflective movement of encountering its own nature.

Mähl argues that Lavater and Franz Hemsterhuis had a notable impact on Novalis's vision of the golden age, given their promotion of enhancing sensory perception and moral instincts (1994: 245). For the Dutch philosopher, the concept of love represented a metaphysical force of global significance, which greatly influenced Novalis. Hemsterhuis integrated Neoplatonic ideas with contemporary science, seeing love as the fundamental drive in all beings to return to a primordial cosmic unity (267-8). The distinction, however, is found in the role of poetry. While Hemsterhuis's passive aesthetic leads him to yearn for an afterlife where the soul might achieve its desired unity, Novalis views poetry as the transformative force that restores this lost unity to the soul. Thus, the golden age is created through the poet's

---

[21] "Die Morgenländerin ist auch die Poesie".
[22] "Die Welt muss romantisiert werden. So findet man den ursprünglichen Sinn wieder".

work (278-81). This transformative poetic action is clearly illustrated in *Ofterdingen*, as will be demonstrated.

Mähl also points to the historical-literary origin of the golden age, tracing it back to Hesiod, and to the fact that Novalis was familiar with this, where "from the suffering of the present and from the attempt to interpret history, the ancient myth of the golden age already emerges, to which Hesiod gave the oldest, literarily tangible form" (3).[23] Above all, Mähl informs us that Novalis was familiar with mythological and classical sources, such as Virgil's eclogues and bucolics or Theocritus's poems (257-60). With different nuances, this promise of a return to an idealized golden age appears in Zoroastrianism, Judaism, Gnosticism, and Christianity, and is present in hermetic writings, configuring this golden image in a profusion of mystical, alchemical, and astrological texts. The ouroboros symbol, the snake that devours itself, is also inscribed in this idea, as it elaborates the eternal return and lost unity. The concept of eternal life realized through the Philosopher's Stone closely aligns with this notion, as the symbolism associated with the Stone's virtues is interconnected with the symbolism of Christ, with both represented in the ouroboros. The character Heinrich learns to master poetry, and this is the synthesis that elevates him to divinity, attracting the golden age to him.

In Fichte's view, the issue of lost unity manifests as an ongoing struggle between intellect and nature, or the self and the non-self: they are inherently connected but remain in perpetual conflict. Ideally, this conflict would be resolved through the diminishing of nature and the elevation of the self to a divine status (Mähl 1994: 284). This represents an alternative way of describing the alchemical merging of opposites, a mystical fusion of contracting and expanding forces that Böhme investigates. In contrast to Hemsterhuis, who advocates for passivity, Fichte promotes self-realization. Novalis supports this view but reframes nature not as a separate entity to be dominated, but as a "thou" that is connected to the self through freedom and love (286).

[23] "aus dem Leiden an der Gegenwart und aus dem Versuch einer Sinndeutung der Geschichte geht bereits der antike Mythos vom goldenen Zeitalter hervor, dem Hesiod die älteste, literarisch faßbare Form gegeben hat".

In Enlightenment thought, as seen in Kant and Lessing's progressive view of History, the present is always considered the pinnacle of progress, while the past represents the most immature stage of humanity. In Novalis's perspective, however, this understanding differs. The highest point is the original state of humanity, and the present should be the link between the past and the future, giving way to innocence and a new childhood (305). Thus, he states that History should transform into *Märchen* (Novalis 1946b: 263) in *Das allgemeine Brouillon*.[24] Thus, the present becomes an absolute present (Mähl 1994: 325).

The *Hymnen an die Nacht* (1800) are a paradigmatic example of Pietist inspiration in Novalis's poetic creation. Furthermore, this inspiration involves a freedom to combine less orthodox beliefs in individual faith. A biographical detail contributed decisively to the mystical journey that composes Novalis's philosophy: the premature death of his beloved fiancée Sophie von Kühn. *Hymnen an die Nacht* follows this transformative loss. Trying not to delve into biographism, there may be a transcendental impact in the fact that his first love has such a significant name for Gnosticism, as it does for the mystical thought of Jacob Böhme, even representing the character Sophia in *Ofterdingen*, a transformative element. Perhaps her death was Novalis's true initiation.

Hymn VI, for example, the last and only one with a title, "Sehnsucht nach dem Tode" [Longing for Death] summarizes the final identification between the deceased beloved, death, and Christ: "the dearest have long rested. [...] / The beloved also long. [...] / Down to the sweet bride, / to Jesus, the beloved" (1945: 24-5).[25] The title, therefore, reveals more than the longing for death; it reveals the chiliastic longing. The golden age, the eternal paradise, is found both in the beloved and in Christ: "to the Father we want to go home, [...] / we must go to the homeland, / to see this holy time" (23-4).[26] And only

---

[24] *Märchen* is a tale that contains elements of the marvellous and also refers to popular narratives with a medieval origin.
[25] "Die Liebsten ruhn schon lange. [...] / Die Lieben sehnen sich wohl auch. [...] / Hinunter zu der süßen Braut, / zu Jesus, dem Geliebten".
[26] "zum Vater wollen wir nach Haus, [...] / wir müssen nach der Heimat gehn, / um diese heilge Zeit zu sehn".

death can remove the barrier that prevents this reunion. The hymns have a close relationship with *Ofterdingen*, in the transcendental dimension of Novalis's work and thought.

Therefore, it is essential to quote Friedrich Schlegel to build the bridge between religion and art: the artist has "a unique religion, an original view of the infinite" (Schlegel 1958: 259).[27] This statement clarifies how alchemy aligns with Novalis's thought and Romanticism itself, as Littlejohns confirms: "Romanticism is, according to the Early Romantics, a mode of describing reality as a symbolic experience, reconfiguring or transfiguring it so that it intimates underlying spiritual or transcendent truths" (2004: 75). Opposites are united: the empirical merges and transmutes into the spiritual through imagination, resulting in a symbolic experience.

In a study on Romanticism and the Natural Sciences, Germanist Gabriele Rommel asserts: "with regard to the history of the sciences and the pre-scientific stages of scientific development such as alchemy, mysticism, and magic, Novalis argued for a symbolic treatment of physics as a poetic treatment of nature" (2004: 218). She points to Egyptian studies and Paracelsus as presented in the work of the physician and botanist Kurt Sprengel, *Versuch einer pragmatischen Geschichte der Arzneikunde* (1794),[28] which Novalis read. She also notes the influence of the astronomer and astrologer Johannes Kepler, whom the poet referred to reverentially as *edler Kepler* (Novalis 1946: 127), meaning "noble Kepler", or "precious" in the case of metals, in *Fragmente des Jahres 1798*. In summary, these studies led Novalis to the conception "of the reciprocal representation of the universe" (2004: 219), the alchemical reciprocal relationship between macrocosm and microcosm.

The same author, in *Geheimnisvolle Zeichen: Alchemie, Magie, Mystik und Natur bei Novalis*, demonstrates that, for Novalis, alchemy was a way of poetizing chemistry (1998: 122) or, extending further, modern science and rational thought. Moreover, Novalis's exploration of alchemy enabled him to develop a comprehensive perspective of the

[27] "eine eigne Religion, eine originelle Ansicht des Unendlichen".
[28] Novalis's work *Die Lehrlinge zu Sais* (1802) recalls this influence of Egypt. Sais is an Egyptian city where the temple of Isis is located.

world, epitomized by the ouroboros, the serpent or dragon devouring its own tail (134). For Novalis, alchemy thus became a teaching of wisdom (136). Mähl supports this interpretation, asserting that Novalis saw the Romantic concept of a universal science as a manifestation of divine revelation within humanity (1994: 240). Comparative literature scholar Beate Allert, writing about Romanticism and the visual arts, confirms that Novalis read Böhme and, furthermore, debated Böhme's ideas with the Romantic painter Otto Runge, who advocated "that everything is contained in everything else throughout the cosmos (*das All-Eine* or the Universal Spirit)" (2004: 286). Both scholars emphasize the same Hermetic themes present in Novalis.

Thus, alchemy becomes a revelation of wisdom. Olivier Schefer, in *Résonances du Romantisme*, notes that for Novalis the origin is chaos, and knowledge is obtained through its organization, contemplation, and synthesis (2005: 30). Romantics aspire to the authentic work of art, *Kunstchaos* (75), the art of chaos, in which chaos, present in both the subject and nature, is liberated through imagination and thought, "in order to extract the potentialities of life" (76).[29] "Extract" is a term from an alchemical poetics that does not content itself with existing material in nature but requires intervention, transforming, destroying, and creating new reality from it. We are not yet in the dissolution of the self into chaos but in the power of the self to reach and order that chaos.

Beyond literary activity, mystical thought and philosophical studies, chemistry also features in Novalis's life. Having worked in mines and saltworks, Novalis studied chemistry, geology, and mathematics. The artistic process of creating *Ofterdingen* is described by the author as "Mischung" [mixture], a term used in chemical studies (Mahoney 2004: 8). In his writings, particularly in the section called "Fremdwörterregister", a "Glossary of Foreign Terms", Novalis draws attention to the definition of *caput mortuum*: "iron oxide; a deep brown-red often used in painting" (1946b: 324).[30] In the seventeenth and eighteenth centuries, the Latin expression is frequently used for both chemistry and painting as a pigment but also to denote alchemical

---

[29] "afin d'en extraire les potentialités de vie".
[30] "Eisenoxyd; ein in der Malerei oft benutztes tiefes Braunrot".

nigredo, representing leftover and disposable residues.

In *Das romantische Paradigma der Chemie Friedrich von Hardenbergs Naturphilosophie* (2003), Liedtke introduces chemistry into the discussion, providing insight into how alchemy was woven into Novalis's life. He explores the convergence of nature philosophy and chemistry, identifying this as the so-called "third way" [*der dritte Weg*]. According to Liedtke, this approach involves seeking the fundamental code of combinatorial art, which merges spirit with matter, or its archetypal form [*Urform*] (2003: 312). This pursuit bears similarities to Goethe's concept of the *Urpflanze* and the restoration of the original androgynous form found in Platonism, Gnosticism, and alchemy. Liedtke also presents a discussion of alchemical themes in the daily press between 1796 and 1802 (2003: 323-78), indicating that Novalis was aware of contemporary chemical and alchemical studies. Indeed, the eighteenth century was a decisive period for the split between chemistry and alchemy. Until the seventeenth century, the disciplines were indistinguishable, with various treatises bearing titles related to chemistry and books on chemistry describing alchemical performances (Principe 2013: 84-7).

From Böhme's readings and Neoplatonic philosophy, Novalis receives the image of a male divinity as the fire element and a female divinity as the light element (Liedtke 2003: 256) and writes in *Neue Notizen* the famous phrase "*Licht macht Feuer*" (1946: 135); light makes fire; the feminine makes the masculine; Sophia creates the material world, revising and inverting the logic of fire as the maker of light.

Mähl reveals Novalis's interest in theosophical secret societies that advocated mystical expression as a stimulus for thought, as well as Hermetic language, which discovered the church within each being (1994: 339-40). Consequently, Novalis likely read Georg von Welling and was interested in the pansophic aspect of knowledge. As evidenced, distinguishing between alchemical influences and mystical, religious, and philosophical influences in Novalis becomes challenging. There is a highly comprehensive synthesis, primarily comprising different strands invoking the same sensual and spiritual power of love. For this reason, Burkhard Dohm, in *Poetische Alchimie*, views Novalis's poetic construction as a treatment of mystical-alchemical transformation models (2000: 365). Novalis's thought shows an intensity in relating philosophies and mystical, religious, and spiritual practices. Alchemy, for Novalis, becomes a philosophy of life.

Dohm notes the extravagant repetition of concepts derived from alchemical and mystical-pietistic experiences, especially the idea of earthly love as the liberator of humanity and the cosmos (365). The researcher mentions Novalis's important alchemical readings: *Alchymia* by Andreas Libavius; *Chimia* by Geber; *Psychosophia or Soul Wisdom* by Johann Joachim Becher; *Chymische Hochzeit* by Johannes Valentinus Andreae; van Helmont; Robert Fludd; Paracelsus; Pordage; Plotinus; Thurneisser; and not only alchemy but also Kabbalah (365-6). As Herbert Uerlings further indicates in *Friedrich von Hardenberg, genannt Novalis*, it is likely that the author also encountered the *Tabula Smaragdina* through Paracelsus (1991: 329).

Giorgio Agamben, discussing alchemical work, concludes that there was "the failure of the Romantic attempt at uniting mystical practice and poetry, work on oneself and the production of a work" (2017: 116). In this regard, Agamben even suggests that Romantic literary production, poetic making, and artistic creation failed to identify the alchemical work with its project. While Agamben's position, as well as ours, remains debatable, reading Novalis, as well as Lord Byron, Percy Bysshe Shelley, Gérard de Nerval, or even the Romantic elements in Goethe, suggests otherwise. This project of uniting writing with mysticism continues with Symbolism (Michaud 1961), Surrealism, and other modernist avant-gardes.

In this sense, we can assert that Novalis was one of the authors who most contributed to the resistance and renewal of alchemy, integrating its theoretical-practical apparatus into Romantic and modern literature. Novalis was one of the authors most read and engaged with by the French intellectual elite of the late nineteenth century, both in poetic and esoteric circles (Michelet 1890). His interest in the charm of the Middle Ages belongs to the mystical-philosophical lineage tracing back to Antiquity with Plotinus, developing in the medieval period with figures like Pseudo-Dionysius the Areopagite, renewed with Marsilio Ficino, consolidated with Paracelsus, and entering Romanticism through Böhme.

Therefore, Novalis's more controversial writings, such as *Die Christenheit oder Europa*, should not be interpreted solely from a Christian and conservative perspective, nor should they be used today to support such a stance. Instead, these works reflect a mystical and poetic fervour, a desire for the rebirth of humanity connected through spirituality, and a renewed appreciation for the marvellous and incomprehensible. Despite Novalis's Christian lenses, his mysticism reveals a struggle against neutral bourgeois empiricism that would undermine the ecstatic nature of artistic creation. Indeed, as we will see in *Ofterdingen*, Novalis attempts to recover a time when humanity deeply experienced nature and read its mysteries as a source of hidden life and meaning.

We will now focus specifically on Novalis's most significant creation, with its alchemical roots.

1.3.3. THE BLUE FLOWER

The alchemical process comprises various stages, each assigned specific colours: *nigredo*, *albedo*, and *rubedo* are the principal stages, associated with black, white and red, respectively. There is also a yellow stage, sometimes a green one, and alchemical texts mention a dark bluish phase occurring after *nigredo*, thus being an early stage. While we will not delve deeply into the different phases of the alchemical process, we will closely examine the often-overlooked nuance of the bluish colour.

Broadly speaking, *nigredo* involves the blackening of matter, searching for the *prima materia* that is part of primordial chaos and the undifferentiated: "*nigredo* or blackness is an initial state, always present at the beginning as a quality of the *prima materia*, of chaos or the confused mass; it can also be produced by the separation of elements (*solutio, separatio, divisio, putrefactio*)" (Jung 1991: 244). Each stage thus has its colour and is organized through different actions. *Nigredo* involves everything related to decomposition, putrefaction, and dissolution of the elements of matter. Following the main sequence, *albedo* addresses the purification of obscured matter, its volatilization and fixation, and its regeneration through its soul in various sublimation processes. As Geber, a prominent Arab alchemist, describes "sublimation with diligent work to remove all impurity that corrupts it. The perfection that sublimation gives to this Stone is to make it so fluid that it reaches the highest purity and fluidity" (Amo *et al.* 1980: 50). Finally, *rubedo* represents the conjunction of all opposites, the true alchemical marriage between white, light, and red, the Sun, culminating in the goals of alchemy, namely, the creation of the Philosopher's Stone. In Jung's psychological understanding, "it corresponds to individuation, the unification of the self. We would say that the stone is a projection of the unified self" (Jung 1988: 161).

In the bluish phase, the black chaos of *nigredo* is contemplated. This phase signifies the transition from decomposition to the regeneration of matter, and is more commonly encountered not as an autonomous phase but as a bluish aspect, such as in flowers, animals, etc. Goethe notes this connection between *nigredo* and the bluish tint of the work: "into the deepest blue, which lies close to black, the colour always increases in darkness" (2016: 141).[31] In his theory of colours, Goethe also states, "[...] that blue always carries something dark with it. [...] As a colour, it is an energy; however, it stands on the negative side and in its highest purity is like a charming nothingness" (179).[32] Blue is the first colour to awaken after the night, before the sun fully illuminates the day. It is that dark blue which still retains the hues of black matter. The colour, as Goethe considers it an energy, finds another meaning in Jung's reflections: "all this was united with the blue quintessence, the *anima mundi* extracted from inert matter" (Jung 1977: 494). In this sense, blue in the alchemical process represents a unifying aspect, emerging from dead, decayed, poisonous, obscure, and chaotic matter, bringing together all elements.

The psychologist James Hillman, founder of archetypal psychology, explored this relationship in *A Blue Fire* (2008) and *Alchemical Psychology* (2010). A phase of the alchemical process seldom mentioned

[31] "In das satteste Blau, das ganz am Schwarzen liegt, nimmt die Farbe immer an Dunkelheit zu".
[32] " [...] dass Blau immer etwas Dunkles mit sich führe. [...] Sie ist als Farbe eine Energie; allein sie steht auf der negativen Seite und ist in ihrer höchsten Reinheit gleichsam ein reizendes Nichts".

in alchemical texts gave Hillman considerable scope to find references affirming the significance of the colour. He asserts that "blue bears traces of the *mortificatio* into the whitening, […] blue protects white from innocence" (2008: 154), referring to the depth of blue in the Madonna's robe and its shadows, reflecting that this purity highlighted is not born from naivety, but from wisdom. Additionally, Hillman connects blue to the transition between *nigredo* and *albedo*, associating the colour with the divine feminine, productive and receptive matter. Jung similarly understands the notion of blue as always associated with the depth of the sky and the sea and with the wisdom of the Gnostic Sophia (2010: 29), a concept developed in the mystical thought of Böhme and later in Novalis. Hillman also describes blue as imagination (31).

Novalis expresses this same conjunction between blue and black and the purity of this relationship in *Ofterdingen* with the phrase "the sky was black-blue and completely pure" (1945: 130).[33] Indeed, blue is a colour frequently used by the author in *Ofterdingen*, as he himself notes in the supplement to the second part of the work, "everything blue in my book" (1945: 334),[34] not only in the infamous flower but also in the described scenery and other objects, such as the veil of the character Sophia (288), who creates a material world while embodying wisdom. Therefore, a book entirely blue, a work entirely blue, implies that everything is transformation and imagination in this work, involving the extraction of inert matter for regeneration and revelation. It is noteworthy that this blue veil appears in a letter Novalis wrote to his mother in 1791, a decade before *Ofterdingen*, in which he refers to "when the blue veil of the future lifts and I see you as the creator of all those bold designs that too bold a confidence dared to place in my abilities" (1946c: 145).[35] The mother is the creator of the son's future projects, behind this blue veil, the wise creator and progenitor, who is also Sophia. For all these reasons, it is not surprising that the flower of Romanticism is blue.

---

[33] "der Himmel war schwarzblau und völlig rein".
[34] "alles blau in meinem Buch".
[35] "Wenn gar der blaue Schleier der Zukunft sich hebt und ich Dich als Schöpferin aller jener kühnen Entwürfe sehe, die eine allzu kühne Zuversicht in meine Kräfte wagte".

From the perspective of innovation and the legacy left to subsequent generations of Romanticism, the most significant aspect is undoubtedly the blue flower, "a model of fantastic expectations destined to be realized" (Mahoney 2004: 16). Its symbolism relates to "the eschatological goal of every mystical journey towards the One" (Navarro 2020: 140).[36] Helmut Gebelein observes that "Novalis, who is regarded by many as a sage conveying hermetic wisdom in his works, clearly drew the Blue Flower of Romanticism in *Heinrich von Ofterdingen* from alchemy" (2000: 238).[37] Considering this hypothesis, where is the blue flower found and what does it symbolize in alchemy?

The blue flower appears in an anonymous treatise, *Pandora*, published by Hieronymus Reussner in 1588 (Roob 2006: 342), which serves as an inspiration for *Ofterdingen* (Rommel 1998: 148). The image in this treatise, which is reproduced on the cover of the present volume, features three flowers: two are white-yellow and red, to the left and right, and one blue with yellow tones in the centre, with a thicker stem, appearing as the main flower from which the other two emerge. The main stem is buried in a circle, coloured blue and yellow, with a red draconian serpent devouring its own tail encircling it. Naturally, this serpent is the ouroboros, an absolute symbol of all alchemy and hermeticism. It is also noted that the tip of the stem is resting on one of the serpent's legs, contaminating the start of the greenish stem with red, suggesting that this is where the flower originates. Below the circle, there is also a moon on the left, a star in the centre, and a sun on the right.

The circle represents the hermetic vessel or philosophical egg, where the *prima materia*, the ouroboros, should be placed to create the Philosopher's Stone. Thus, this egg symbolizes birth and transformation, which occur in matter in the presence of the three essential substances found in everything: mercury, salt, and sulphur. In this hermetic vessel, the aim is to recreate the origin of world formation, as nature did from chaos and undifferentiated matter, marked by the

[36] "La meta escatológica de todo viaje místico hacia lo Uno".
[37] "Novalis, der vielen als ein Weiser gilt, der in seinen Werken hermetische Weisheiten mitteilt. Die Blaue Blume der Romantik in Heinrich von Ofterdingen ist ganz eindeutig aus der Alchemie entnommen".

ouroboros. This is the alchemical purpose, although a quicker and more perfected transformation than that of nature itself is sought. Jung also discusses the blue flower, the sapphire of the hermaphrodite, better known as the alchemical gold flower (1972: 101), which too appears as a white and red rose in the alchemical treatises of George Ripley (*Ripley Scroll*, 1588) and Robert Fludd (*Summum Bonum*, 1629).

The two roses, white and red, refer to lunar and solar tinctures, respectively. The tincture provides the power of transmutation, rejuvenation, and life extension, according to Paracelsus (1894: 28-9), aligning with a return to a golden age, a union with nature, and the origin of primordial Adam. The tincture results from the passage of three essences into one, which may also be called the lily of alchemy (22). For this transformation, the tincture must first undergo the process of blackening (27). Thus, it appears that the lateral flowers in *Pandora* merge into the central blue flower: the union of lunar and solar, giving rise to the hermetic androgyne or hermaphrodite, which we will discuss shortly, as the primordial origin of human consciousness. In *Pandora*, Pandora is described as the Philosopher's Stone and the Earth Mother (Szulakowska 2017: 112), which might correspond to the character Fabula in Klingsohr's *Märchen*, as I will argue, embodying both creation and creator. This dual role hints at a key idea: the Hermetic hermaphrodite and the Philosopher's Stone represent the same state of consciousness and perfection.[38]

The three flowers arise from the ouroboros egg. Devouring its own tail is an auto-fecundating and transmuting act, which leads back to a primitive, more authentic, and thus more real state of "primitive and perhaps future union of the universal family of stone, plant, animal, and man" (Marques 1947: 47). However, this unity is not a given but a tense relationship, a return that must be actively pursued, as I will attempt to demonstrate, and which Heinrich will ultimately achieve. Carl Seelig, editor of the collected works of Novalis, comments that

---

[38] The alchemical origin of the blue flower does not exclude its Indian ancestry. For Novalis, Sanskrit was the language that contained "the secrets of the universe, and among the mysteries he invoked was the symbolism of the Blaue Blume" (Thapar 2011: 211). The story of the young Shakuntala was well-known to Novalis. Cf. Figueira 1991: 13.

Novalis, through pantheistic mysticism, arrives at magical idealism, in which he conceives God as power in action in every being (cf. 1945b: 74). The self's unity with nature constitutes divinity and is inscribed in "the living image of an Ouroboros Snake, a uroproctological *hen-to pan* [...] symbol" (Ceronetti 1993: 36). Indeed, the expression *hen-to pan*, "the all is one", appears within the circle formed by the snake in the alchemical treatise *Chrysopoeia of Cleopatra*.

The longing and desire for this unity, the German word "*Sehnsucht*", is represented in the quest for the blue flower. As Ralf Liedtke asserts, "*Ofterdingen* is the literary paragon of the awakening of hermetic "*Sehnsucht*" (1996: 27). In alchemy, this unity occurs through the conjunction of opposites, and the union of the self and the universe, of the microcosm and the macrocosm, even if not opposed, represents a tense search. The *anima mundi*, the blue quintessence, extracted from inert matter, contemplates the whole as belonging to the soul of the world, where matter and imagination meet.

The universal family evokes the Aristotelian immanentist tradition and Spinoza: what exists permeates being, and nothing is external in creation. Thus, the macrocosm is a mirror of the microcosm, and vice versa, not being transcendentally separated from it, as taught by the first alchemical law, inscribed in the *Tabula Smaragdina*, legendarily written by the father of alchemy, Hermes Trismegistus: "What is below is like that which is above, and what is above is like that which is below, to accomplish the miracles of the One" (Roob 2006: 9). In this sense, the relationship with nature cannot be one of domination but of contemplation.

The poet is superior because he relates to nature as it is, without subjugating it. For this reason, Heinrich's path will be to encounter his vocation as a poet, "the purest revelation of humanity" (Marques 1947: 47), and it is the message of revelation that alchemy carries within its womb, uniting the different mystical and religious currents. To be a poet is, in sum, to return to the archetypal man, the primordial hermaphroditic being, created from the "word of love" (47). Novalis wrote in *Blütenstaub* that "Poets and priests were one in the beginning" (1945: 25),[39] because they heal, illuminate, reveal, unite, and transform

[39] "Dichter und Priester waren im Anfang eins".

like a true alchemist. This conception implies the Romantic vision of the genius, which, in the words of Wolfgang Beutin *et al.*, in *A History of German Literature*, concerns "magnifying subjective and irrational elements to the point of deifying art and the creative artist" (1993: 171).

The golden flower of alchemy is the blue flower; that is, the sought-after gold is wisdom. This wisdom is revealed from within, and thus Heinrich must walk in that direction. It is the same *Weg nach Innen* [Journey Inward] of Novalis, in *Blütenstaub*, hence Jung states, in *Das symbolische Leben*, that this flower is the symbol of the experience of the psyche in Romanticism and alchemy (1981: 834). In *Poetizismen*, Novalis reflects this projection from the micro to the macrocosm, writing: "we are God's children, divine seeds. One day we will be what our Father is" (1946: 42).[40] This inward path recalls the alchemical aphorism *ambula ab intra*, journey from within, invoked by the esoteric philosopher Julius Evola in *La tradizione ermetica* (2006: 53), from the anonymous treatise *De Pharmaco Catholico*.

The change from within is the path of the alchemists. Alchemical principles are drawn from within the alchemist. The true Stone is found within the self or is the self itself. The gold to be discovered reveals itself within. Alchemical transmutation is the transformation of the human being. The transmuted being heeds their vocation as the messiah of nature, the one who "always expressed the symbolic philosophy of his being in his works" (Novalis 1946: 220),[41] as written in *Das allgemeine Brouillon*.

Now that the image of the blue flower and its alchemical symbolism has been examined, we can begin to read *Heinrich von Ofterdingen*.

[40] "Gotteskinder, göttliche Keime sind wir. Einst werden wir sein, was unser Vater ist".

[41] " […] hat immer symbolische Philosophie seines Wesens in seinen Werken […] ausgedrückt".

2

HEINRICH, THE ALCHEMIST POET

Heinrich von Ofterdingen was conceived in 1799 but remained unfinished at Novalis's premature death in 1801. The first complete part, along with fragments and ideas for the second part, were posthumously published in 1802, under the care of the Romantic author Ludwig Tieck. It is pertinent to note that the open-ended nature of the work is "a common feature of Romanticism – with *Heinrich von Ofterdingen* being a key example" (Mahoney 2004: 18). Curiously, and much in line with the hermetic tradition, the first part, *Erwartung* [Expectation], is complete, contrasting with the second part, *Erfüllung* [Fulfilment], which, ironically, and also characteristic of Romanticism, was left incomplete. However, it could be said that the open ending of the first part sustains a state of expectation, while the fragmentary nature of the second part embodies an accidental Romantic intention, aligning Novalis's unfinished work with the thematic and stylistic ideals of the Romantic movement.

Regarding the thematic structure of the work, Novalis explicitly aimed to respond to Goethe's works *Wilhelm Meisters Lehrjahre* and *Märchen*, published in 1795, creating a mixed genre of novel and tale, *Roman* and *Märchen*, with an emphasis on the formation of the self, the well-known *Bildungsroman* [formation novel], so that the protagonist's potential would be fulfilled. As Uerlings clarifies, *Wilhelm Meisters Lehrjahre* has been established as the most important paradigm for investigating *Ofterdingen*, as Novalis studied this novel thoroughly, initially with enthusiasm and later with harsh criticism. However, a sort of subjugation to the master Goethe and the use of *Lehrjahre* as a paradigm have blocked, at the time of Uerlings' study, other possible readings of *Ofterdingen* (1991: 402). While it is true that there are certain formal formulae reminiscent of Goethe's, it is also important to note that the journey of Goethe's character differs from that of Novalis.

Instead of starting in a dream world, aware of an artistic vocation, ending with the protagonist's social engagement like Wilhelm Meister, Heinrich departs from a real world to a dreamed one. There is, therefore, an inversion of the path taken by Goethe's project, as Novalis's primary interest lay in the relationship between poetic vocation and the opening of the finite to the infinite. Indeed, as Allen Speight notes, citing Schlegel's work *Europa* (1803: 56), it is a case of "Schlegel's own typological distinction between 'exoteric' and 'esoteric' novels (the former, like *Wilhelm Meisters Lehrjahre*, representing the ideal of the beautiful in everyday life, and the latter, like *Heinrich von Ofterdingen*, offering a 'transition from novel to mythology')" (2020: 312).

Ofterdingen is considered by Marcel Brion to be an endless journey. In *L'Allemagne romantique*, the author reflects that in *Ofterdingen*, everything is an endless journey (1962: 80). The reasons are mainly two: the fragmentary and unfinished nature of the book and, more importantly, the transformative action carried out by the characters and what they represent. The flower that metamorphoses, the journey that recounts other journeys, the dream that dreams other dreams, and even the characters that unfold, being many and one, as I intend to show. Indeed, if the blue flower symbolizes the mystical journey to the one, the prime matter and origin of things, the incompletion of *Ofterdingen* shows how inaccessible this one can be.

The fact that the alchemical process seems never to end is ultimately recorded in the conception of perfection and the Philosopher's Stone for each alchemist and scholar. However, the fragment conveys this image of incompleteness, being complete in its impossibility to expand further. Like Heinrich's dream or Klingsohr's tale, the end of the fragment is unpredictable for the reader: it can conclude abruptly, without prior indication, and still make perfect sense. The alchemical work represents this very idea, the alchemist realizing that there is always something more to be calcined, transmuted and sublimated. It tends towards an open ending, but not an inconclusive one. And even when it seems that an end has been reached, there are still phases such as *multiplicatio* and *projectio*, which, after the *rubedo*, amplify, multiply, and project the transmutation process into all other beings. As I will note, Heinrich does not limit himself to fulfilling the vocation of a poet; he consumes poetry and projects it into external reality until everything becomes tale and poetry.

The recognition of this infinite task is well-present in Novalis's thought. For example, in his poem "Kenne dich selbst" ["Know Thyself"], we understand that the absolute, always longed for, is within us, but it is a mistake to try to know the absolute absolutely:

> One thing only is what mankind has sought through all times;
> Everywhere, sometimes on the heights, sometimes in the depths of
> the world –
> Under various names – fruitlessly – it has always remained hidden.
> Always he felt it near – yet he never grasped it.
> Long ago there was a man who, in friendly myths to children,
> Revealed the path and key to the hidden castle.
> Few could decipher the simple cipher of the solution,
> But those few also became masters of the destination.
> Long ages passed – error sharpened our senses –
> So that the myth no longer concealed the truth from us.
> Blessed is he who has become wise and no longer digs the world,
> Who desires the stone of eternal wisdom within himself.
> Only the rational man is the true adept – he transforms
> Everything into life and gold – he no longer needs elixirs.
> In him steams the holy alembic – the king is within him –
> Delphi too, and he finally comprehends this: Know thyself.
>   (Novalis 1945b: 103)[1]

[1] "Eins nur ist, was der Mensch zu allen Zeiten gesucht hat;
Überall, bald auf den Höhn, bald in den Tiefen der Welt –
Unter verschiedenen Namen – umsonst – es versteckte sich immer,
Immer empfand er es nah – dennoch erfasst er es nie.

According to Novalis, the highest we can achieve is not meaning but feeling—specifically, the capacity for transcendental perception, beyond time and space. Yet, as Yu Takahashi notes,

> Novalis considers the alchemical attempt to "transform everything into life and gold" through elixirs as an "error"; on the other hand, he also recognizes that "the error sharpened our senses." While the possibility of finding the Absolute in the spatiotemporal world is excluded, the attempt is a necessary process for self-knowledge. (2008: 94)[2]

Thus, it is not the importance of the process itself but, above all, the significance of error. Alchemy is an experimental science that contemplates and operates within the realm of error.

Furthermore, the poem demonstrates Novalis's profound understanding of alchemy by identifying the Philosopher's Stone with both the self and the blue flower, in this invocation to the Delphic oracle. The Stone and the flower represent quests for the absolute, for the One. Uerlings also argues that the poem reflects Novalis's attitude toward alchemy, which he had been studying since 1797, revealing

Längst schon fand sich ein Mann – der den Kindern in freundlichen Mythen
Weg und Schlüssel verriete zu des Verborgenen Schloss
Wenige deuteten sich die leichte Chiffre der Lösung
Aber die Wenigen auch waren nun Meister des Ziels.
Lange Zeiten verflossen – der Irrthum schärfte den Sinn uns –
Dass uns der Mythus selbst nicht mehr die Wahrheit verbarg.
Glücklich, wer weise geworden und nicht die Welt mehr durchgrübelt,
Wer von sich selber den Stein ewiger Weisheit begehrt.
Nur der vernünftige Mensch ist der ächte Adept – er verwandelt
Alles in Leben und Gold – braucht Elixiere nicht mehr.
In ihm dampfet der heilige Kolben – der König ist in ihm –
Delphos auch und er fasst endlich das: Kenne dich Selbst."
[2] "Den alchemistischen Versuch, 'Alles in Leben und Gold' durch Elixiere zu verwandeln, beurteilt Novalis einerseits als 'Irrthum', andererseits erkennt er aber auch, 'der Irrthum schärfte den Sinn uns'. Die Möglichkeit, in der raum-zeitlichen Welt das Absolute zu finden, ist zwar ausgeschlossen, aber der Versuch ist ein notwendiger Prozess für die Selbsterkenntnis."

three paths to the One: through myths, practical alchemy and its elixirs, and self-knowledge (1991: 249). As initially discussed, the idea of having a king within each of us is also present here. This king represents the complete knowledge of our capabilities and actions; it is to be a true adept, that is, a novice in the Real Art, a term used for the practice of alchemy.

A clear and fundamental summary of the meaning of *Heinrich von Ofterdingen* can be found in Mahoney's words: "a dream of the blue flower that inspires the protagonist to undertake a search destined to transform the entire world into a realm ruled by love, peace, and poetry" (2004: 7). Hence the influence of the self-transformative dream that guides the protagonist in changing the world begins with an inward-moving axipetal shift and is followed by an outward-moving axifugal shift, or as Novalis writes in *Blütenstaub*, "the mysterious path goes inward. [...] The second step must be a more effective gaze outward" (1945b: 13-5).[3] The alchemist transmutes himself to transmute the world, to exercise *multiplicatio* and *projectio*.

For Novalis, the superior genius of the poet is found in his metaphorical suicidal capacity (Marques 1947: 48). Suicide is, in a sense, akin to self-combustion, a self-devouring movement, reminiscent of a revelatory dream recounted by the alchemist Zosimos:

> I saw a sacrificer standing before me, atop an altar shaped like a cup. [...] The priest stood there, and I heard a voice from above saying to me: "I have accomplished the act of descending the fifteen steps, walking toward darkness, and the act of ascending the steps, moving toward light. It is the sacrificer who renews me, by rejecting the dense nature of the body. Thus consecrated as a priest by necessity, I become a spirit." (Berthelot 1888: 117-8)[4]

[3] "Nach Innen geht der geheimnisvolle Weg. [...] Der zweite Schritt muss wirksamer Blick nach aussen".
[4] "Je vis un sacrificateur qui se tenait debout devant moi, en haut d'un autel en forme de coupe. [...] Le prêtre s'y tenait debout, et j'entendis une voix d'en haut qui me disait: 'J'ai accompli l'action de descendre les quinze

Between the sacrificer and the priest, this person, in Zosimos's vision, undergoes the transformation from body to spirit through sublimation: purging what is dense, heavy, "the dense nature of the body", which can also be impure, in order to extract what is gaseous, light, and volatile—the spirit. The steps described by Zosimos could represent the number of times his master was reincarnated. First, it is necessary to descend in order to ascend: the eschatological journey represented by the previously mentioned blue flower. Dionysus descended into the underworld later to be reborn, as did Christ, Orpheus, Achilles, Ulysses, Dante, and many others. All underwent this initiation of killing the body to become spirit, or in other words, purging density to obtain the knowledge which, as previously mentioned, is salvation. As Carl Jung suggests in *Psychology and Alchemy*, the ups and downs in these steps reflect the highs and lows of psychic transformation (1972: 83).

This dismemberment also happened to Zosimos's master, as he recounts to his disciple:

> Someone came […] and he assaulted me, striking me with a sword, dismembering me. […] He removed all the skin from my head with the sword he held (in hand); he mixed the bones with the flesh and made them burn with the fire of the treatment. (Berthelot 1888: 118)[5]

After recounting what happened to him, Zosimos "vomited all his flesh [and] (changed into) a little deformed man" (118).[6] Vomiting one's own flesh evokes the ouroboros: eternal return, union of opposites,

marches, en marchant vers l'obscurité, et l'action de monter les marches, en allant vers la lumière. C'est le sacrificateur qui me renouvelle, en rejetant la nature épaisse du corps. Ainsi consacré prêtre par la nécessité, je deviens un esprit.'"

[5] "Quelqu'un est venu […] et il m'a violenté, me pourfendant avec un glaive, en me démembrant. […] Il a enlevé toute la peau de ma tête, avec l'épée qu'il tenait (en main); il a mêlé les os avec la chair et il les a fait brûler avec le feu du traitement".

[6] "Vomit toutes ses chairs [et] (changé en) petit homme contrefait".

transformation, and self-fecundation. For this reason, this act makes him become that little "deformed" man: misshapen, simulated, artificial. Carl Jung suggests in *On the Psychology of Western and Eastern Religion* that the reference to this little man is the first reference to the homunculus, the human created in a laboratory and alchemically, and that this is how Zosimos perceives himself. In his psychic transformation, his unconscious produces the image of him as an incomplete, stunted man made of a poor material, like lead or copper, far from silver and gold. *Divisio, separatio*, and *solutio* might represent the stages Zosimos is undergoing (Jung 1963: 246-7), stages that allude to dismemberment. The path is always aimed at the reconstitution of the whole: "all things proceed from unity and return to unity" (Berthelot 1888: 390),[7] or, "you know that: One is the Whole and from the Whole comes the Whole" (170).[8]

Moreover, Novalis's poetic genius's suicidal capacity also reflects the Christian mystical interpretation of Kirchweger in his treatise *Aurea Catena Homeri* (1723) of the transition from earthly to heavenly nature through the blood of Christ: to die in order to be reborn in the primordial waters, to return to the prime matter, involves a cyclical and self-consuming process, where the subject consumes himself or another human substance, "the transformation of his own earthly nature into a heavenly nature by means of a true rebirth through the blood of Christ" (Kirchweger 2016: 43). In perceiving the self as the material to be transmuted, suicide is the act of the alchemist performing on himself, starting with his *nigredo*. Thus, the suicidal capacity is a self-creating and ouroboric ability, as the serpent devours itself, that is, recreates itself. The suicidal movement is not only directed inward but also reconfigures the external world; a movement inward and another outward. After the inner transmutation, conditions are created for the external transmutation. Two opposing movements that aim to be one, in order to obtain the absolute reality of poetry. Let us now observe how everything processes in *Heinrich von Ofterdingen*.

---

[7] "Toutes choses procèdent de l'unité et se rangent dans l'unité".

[8] "Tu sais que: Un est le Tout et que du Tout naît le Tout".

It is night, and a beam of moonlight illuminates Heinrich's room. His thoughts are preoccupied with what a certain stranger had told him. His greatest yearning is to discover the blue flower, "not the treasures" (1945: 127),[10] and whenever the image of this flower fades in his mind, the ecstasy dissipates, giving way to "a deep, intimate bustling activity" (127-8).[11] The image of the old alchemist, seeking material wealth and turning everything into gold, does not resonate with Heinrich's aspirations, nor does the pursuit of purely rational and bookish knowledge. The stranger evokes the unknown, a product of the irrational, and the obsession with the blue flower, as the most valuable treasure to pursue, serves as an elusive ideal rather than an achievable reality.

Heinrich's life is driven by dreams. As he notes: "it is as if I had just dreamt, or as if I had drifted into another world; for in the world I used to live in, who would have cared about flowers?" (127).[12] There is an inherent despair in Heinrich, driven by the fact that this stranger occupies his mind and the blue flower, whose intermittent image—sometimes present, sometimes faded—both enthrals and disturbs him. This despair is rooted in Heinrich's life drive, evident in his yearning for the unknown, a belief that the world is on the verge of returning to a primitive time when animals, plants, and stones communicated with people, and that this is the revelation the stranger is showing him (1945: 128). The idea of a universal family, previously mentioned, merges with the revelation and the messianic vocation of nature. Indeed, this yearning is life-affirming and creative.

The work begins in the night, marking the start of the writing of his life's story, the end of the world as he knows it, and the beginning of a new life. In *Ofterdingen*, the *nigredo* acquires a new definition of

---

[9] The practice of alchemy is also known as the Royal Art, Alchemical Art, or the *Magnum Opus*, the Great Work.

[10] "nicht die Schätze".

[11] "ein tiefes, inniges Treiben".

[12] "es ist, als hätt ich vorhin geträumt, oder ich wäre in eine andere Welt hinübergeschlummert; denn in der Welt, in der ich sonst lebte, wer hätte da sich um Blumen bekümmert".

alchemical death. More accurately, Heinrich's reaction to the need to enter the first stage of transmutation is one of surrender to this death, a suicidal step. Hence, the stranger who appears to Heinrich, and whom Heinrich later concludes to be "a resident of the higher world" (178),[13] offers him the thought of the blue flower, more desired than any treasure, and the possibility of reconnecting with that mythical time of unity with nature. The stranger, in turn, lacks form—no face, name, or dialogue—perhaps because, as a product of Heinrich's unconscious, it symbolizes an ideal state of harmony and resolution. This state represents the potential reconciliation of humanity with nature and the self with the cosmos. Although Heinrich has a long journey ahead, he is marked to be initiated into the mysteries of nature.

Heinrich falls asleep thinking: "there must be many words that I do not know: if I knew more, I could understand everything much better" (128).[14] His desire to communicate with all these forms of nature leads him to an absolute language, and it is through poetry that the protagonist will discover all these unknown words. Heinrich wishes to master the logocentric tool. While he will learn it, he will always belong to the symbol and image, the synthesis of dream, tale, and poetry itself. The word is not his means of accessing knowledge, but imagination; as we will discover. To achieve this, he must learn the balance between reason and intuition.

Novalis's poetic philosophy intersects with hermetic philosophy when he asserts in *Neue Notizen*, "poetry is the truly absolute reality. This is the core of my philosophy. The more poetic, the truer" (1946: 141).[15] This confirms that the poet is a "second god" (Marques 1947: 51),[16] and so is the alchemist: alchemical language possesses a

---

[13] "ein Bewohner der höheren Welt".

[14] "es muss noch viel Worte geben, die ich nicht weiß: wusste ich mehr, so könnte ich viel besser alles begreifen".

[15] "Die Poesie ist das echt absolut Reelle. Dies ist der Kern meiner Philosophie. Je poetischer, je wahrer".

[16] Schiller shared this idea, as did Goethe, all of whom owe something to Spinoza. Schiller considers that God conceived a world when creating it, and that human beings, by thinking, create their own world. Moreover, God and

demiurgic power, as does poetic language. More than making his poetry the contemplation of the absolute realm of love, Heinrich integrates within himself, as both alchemist and poet, Novalis's transformative poetic operations. Like a primary deity who exists because of what he created, Heinrich must learn the words that allow him to create unity with things.

The language created becomes autonomous to generate its creators and transform reality. This is why poetry is so essential to Heinrich and why he will learn it from his beloved's father: "é um itinerário de amor e pelo amor. Poesia é a realização do amor" (51),[17] just as alchemy presents itself in its various stages. It is the path to divine wisdom, Gnostic Sophia, the awareness of all creation. Returning to the primordial hermaphrodite is a return to wholeness. Making the primordial Adam return to Sophia, alchemically uniting the real pair, or joining the head of the serpent to its tail are realizations of love, the force of expansion, in Böhme.

What seems important is to relate the nature that the alchemist and the poet are trying to recreate with wisdom and love; we will address the latter later. Böhme, in his theosophy, demonstrates how crucial nature is to understand the great mystery of alchemy, the concept of *Mysterium Magnum*. He conceives two substances within this mystery: the manifestation of divinity through the unity and wisdom inherent in the universe, a self-awareness that makes the universe understand itself as god; and nature itself, which, though not united with god, is always in motion, driven by a desire for unity with him (1991: 24). If the *Mysterium Magnum* consists of these two substances, then it is also chaos (25), the confluence of good and evil, the mouth and tail of the serpent.

As an heir to various dual traditions, Böhme observes the duality between the unity of wisdom and the movement of non-unity. We also note that, for Böhme, wisdom, inheriting from the Kabbalah, is the knowledge of the divine to the point of becoming one with it. This is

Nature are identified with each other. Cf. Victor Delbos, *O problema moral na filosofia de Spinoza e na história do spinozismo* (Rio de Janeiro: FGV, 2017), 284.

[17] "é um itinerário de amor e pelo amor. Poesia é a realização do amor".

the direction Heinrich will follow. Novalis views poetry as an operation that accelerates the spiritual process, a transformative and creative movement that will spiritually advance the poet. This helps us understand the alchemical mark of continuous transmutation towards the perfect wisdom of the universe.

Heinrich dreams all night, and these dreams present the necessary trans-formations he must undergo. Many adventures are experienced during this night:

> He first dreamed of unappealing distances and wild, unknown regions. He wandered over seas with incomprehensible ease; he saw marvellous animals; he lived among diverse people [...]. He fell into captivity and the most disgraceful hardship. All sensations rose to an unprecedented height within him. He experienced an infinitely colourful life; died and returned, loved with the highest passion, and was then forever separated from his beloved. (1945: 128)[18]

The *nigredo* announced by the night, in which his story begins to be narrated, gains strength in this dream. The past trials represent the calcination and putrefaction necessary to proceed with the dissolution of the elements, their separation, with the aim of reducing them to their essence and then reuniting them in the greatest of passions. Alchemically, it would be to separate the volatile from the fixed and then recombine them. In the dream, he undergoes a colourful life, a reference to the various colours of the alchemical phases, the so-called *cauda pavonis*, and dies and resurrects, *nigredo* and *albedo*. Once the volatile and fixed elements are reunited, a first conjunction occurs.

---

[18] "Da träumte ihm erst von unansehnlichen Fernen und wilden, unbekannten Gegenden. Er wanderte über Meere mit unbegreiflicher Leichtigkeit; wunderliche Tiere sah er; er lebte mit mannigfaltigen Menschen [...]. Er geriet in Gefangenschaft und die schmählichste Not. Alle Empfindungen stiegen bis zu einer nie gekannten Höhe in ihm. Er durchlebte ein unendlich buntes Leben; starb und kam wieder, liebte bis zur höchsten Leidenschaft und war dann wieder auf ewig von seiner Geliebten getrennt".

This ends in a second separation, a new *nigredo*, so that the elements can be purified and improved once more. All of this is a process of self-discovery and self-knowledge, translated alchemically.

Still dreaming, Heinrich crosses a dark forest. However, this crossing is already occurring at dawn, whether this part of the day is in the world outside the dream or within the dream itself. Here, there is polarity: the dawn, the rising aurora, against the dark forest. The gathering of the first dew of the day, which marks the beginning of the alchemical work, i.e., the transformations, still before the clear light of *albedo*, still in the bluish phase. The forest is a place of rebirth, of initiation. With this dawn, a scant light begins to enter the greenery, the "green net" (945: 128) of the dark forest,[19] which remains a location of the unconscious. Therefore, the process of purification, of rebirth, after the second *nigredo*, begins to take place, and perhaps, this greenery of the forest could be associated with the *viriditas*, the green phase, which also symbolizes the adept's rebirth. This is reinforced by Heinrich's ascent up a slope of mossy stones, and as he climbs higher, the forest becomes less dense until he finds himself in a small meadow at the foot of a mountain, which once again symbolizes initiation.

Johannes Valentinus Andreae's alchemical treatise, *Die chymische Hochzeit von Christian Rosenkreutz* (1616), presents the main character, Rosenkreutz, who also begins his story at night and receives an invitation to attend a royal wedding (the king and queen, the alchemical royal pair). His journey also takes him through a forest, where he encounters the first of three mountains, entering it to receive a golden insignia marking the completion of the first stage (1973: 52-57). Heinrich discovers a carved entrance and proceeds towards it, from which an intense and clear light emanates. One could say that this light corresponds to Rosenkreutz's golden insignia.

This light originates from a golden beam that pours forth, and the cave itself is lined with this light. The sparks from this stream of light collect in a basin. Heinrich dips his hand into it, brings his hand to his lips, and feels a "spiritual breath" (1945: 129).[20] His energy is

---

[19] "grünes Netz".
[20] "geistiger Hauch".

rejuvenated, leading him to undress and bathe in the golden light as if surrounded by "a cloud of the sunset" (129).[21] It is in this solar tincture that Heinrich bathes, gaining new strength and vitality, perfecting himself. The evening glow lends a reddish-golden hue to the light. Although the light is not entirely purple, it, as a material, takes on the yellow form of the operation, *citrinitas*, the awakening.

The spiritual breath he feels when placing his hand in the light may invoke what Böhme describes in *Aurora* when a spark ignites the heart: it first shines, but when the source of the heart awakens, it is as if the spark is blown and explodes into flames (2013: 298). The breath in the spark ignites the heart, with fire and calcination operating within Heinrich. The gathering of light sparks in the basin may also refer to Böhme. Not only because of the reddish-golden title, *Aurora*, but also due to the construction of a similar image in which the basin that collects all the particles of light is God, the final vocation. All the particles represent all created beings, as each being has a spark of divine light (2013: 141; 166). Novalis uses the same word as Böhme, "der Funke" [the spark], and Heinrich is yet another spark joining in this bath of light, becoming light itself, i.e., belonging to the One.

Fire and light play a significant role in Böhme's thought, as we have seen, and clearly in Novalis's as well. For Böhme, fire represents natural life, while light represents sacred life and unity (1991: 24). We recall Novalis's expression, mentioned earlier as inheriting from Böhme: "Licht macht Feuer" (light makes fire), where light, the sacred, and unity create the natural world. In Böhme's conception, this light gives rise to a fire of love: "this burning Fire is but a manifestation of Life, and of the Divine Love, by which the Divine Love, namely the unity kindles up, and sharpens itself for the fiery working of the power of God" (24-25). The alchemical tradition always sees fire as life itself, the exercise of the manifestation of the divine and light.

However, fire also signifies the transformation of matter, allowing its reorganization and rebirth in a new purified form. Indeed, everything we know about fire can be metaphorized in the alchemical process and, as we will see, in Heinrich's process. Fire burns for only a

[21] "eine Wolke des Abendrots".

64

certain period. It is not eternal light; it is a manifestation, and like all manifestations of the divine, it is bound by time. Excessive fire destroys the work, while insufficient fire prevents it from continuing. Light itself can blind or even burn, as illustrated by the myth of the destruction of Semele, the last mortal mother of Dionysus, who perished upon seeing Zeus in his divine form. Thus, we are reminded once again of alchemy as a science of error: how to determine the right amount of fire other than through the experience of creation. In due course, we will see how this unfolds for Heinrich.

Inside the basin, or rather, the philosopher's egg, voluptuousness [*Wollust*] overwhelms his heart, and images merge in his thoughts, creating feminine forms that appear to him like a deluge [*Flut*] (1945: 129). We might interpret this as Heinrich's awakening of sexual life, and even consider the burst of light and the deluge of feminine images as a nocturnal ejaculatory act. As Ronald Gray attests, "there is in fact a sexual element in all alchemical writings" (2010: 17). The first alchemy is the creation of life, the initial alchemical exercise of recreating the work of nature in the creation of the world. Böhme's principles are aligned with those of Fichte's idealism: there is a dynamic divine principle that creates both spirit and matter. However, this principle does not exclude matter from non-being. On the contrary, matter is necessary as a manifestation of the divine. Fire is needed for light to manifest.

This solar bath of Heinrich must contain the dew that liquefies the light. This deluge of liquefied feminine images constitutes, in the absence of another physical body, the mercurial water, *aqua sapientiae*, the lunar pole that Heinrich desires to attract. Paracelsus helps relate this dew to Heinrich's sensations and images. The alchemist cites another, Salmanazar, who refers to a humid fire that forms "an air like a cloud", i.e., "dew of chaos", "moisture of the cloud" (1976: 70). Furthermore, Paracelsus reflects on the elixir that preserves bodies from corruption, made from dew (1894: 74), which he also calls the "flower of the Air" (367). These images that merge into each other [*ineinanderflossen*] in Heinrich are thus dew of chaos, moisture of the cloud, that *Wolke des Abendrots*, which, in summary, combines cloud, air, light, red, and yellow. In essence, Heinrich's dream reveals the desire for the conjunction of opposites, the *coincidentia oppositorum* of alchemy, the union of dualities, one of the major projects of German Romanticism.

In this ecstasy, Heinrich dreams that he falls into drowsiness and dreams that he dreams. From the example of Zosimus, we see that the device of dreaming is widely used in alchemical treatises as a means of initiation and liberation of the mind in order to learn the path to be followed. Similarly, the *Corpus Hermeticum*, a pillar of Hermeticism, alchemy, and Gnosticism, allegedly written by Thoth himself, the Egyptian Hermes, begins with someone falling asleep and dreaming of a being named Poimandres, who presents himself as the *Nous*, the mental faculty to contemplate eternal and immutable things in a Platonic sense, among many other definitions less relevant to this context. What matters is that there is a mystagogical quality, a necessity of initiation. We also recall another dream of Zosimus:

> I perceived during my sleep a certain small man, […] and he said to me: What are you doing (there), oh man? And I replied: I am stopping here because, having strayed from all paths, I find myself lost. He then said to me: Follow me. And I went and followed him. […] I saw the one who was guiding me, […] enter this place, and his entire body was consumed by fire. (Berthelot 1888: 125)[22]

Fire is the constant element in the work and the accounts, whether to dissolve, to unite, or simply to keep the operation ongoing. This fiery man is Zosimus' guide.

In this dream within Heinrich's dream, he experiences "indescribable events [...], another enlightenment" (1945: 130).[23] This enlightenment bridges the previous dream of the light bath, reminiscent of Zosimos' dream, to the next dream—or rather, the continuation of the same dream—suggesting he is within the luminous basin as he dreams it. As

[22] "J'aperçus pendant mon sommeil un certain petit homme, […] et il me dit: Que fais-tu (là), ô homme? Et moi je lui répondis: Je m'arrête ici parce que, m'étant écarté de tout chemin, je me trouve égaré. Il me dit alors: Suis-moi. Et moi, je vins et je le suivis. […] je vis celui qui me guidait, […] s'engager dans ce lieu et tout son corps fut consumé par le feu."

[23] "unbeschreibliche Begebenheiten […], eine andere Erleuchtung".

Uerlings reflects, based on Mahoney's studies, the action of light alludes to the Vulcanist theory, which posits that the Earth's internal fire shapes its current external form. Regardless, fire is mystagogical. This lava light activates Heinrich's next dream, creating nature as a product of the forces of love: "the mutual penetration of self and nature" (1991: 413).[24] This signifies the romantic reconciliation of the Fichtean project.

In a setting of bluish rocks with multicoloured veins under a dark bluish sky, Heinrich lies in a meadow beside a spring, captivated by a luminous blue flower, touching it gently. This sequence seems to highlight the transformation: the two roses, red and white, the solar and lunar tinctures, Heinrich in the golden-rubified light, and the liquefied feminine forms around him, have led to this blue flower. Therefore, it could only appear in a different dream, a dream resulting from another dream, like a flower that blooms from another flower. Its petals lean towards Heinrich, forming a blue collar and revealing a face as the flower undergoes a metamorphosis, until the protagonist is awakened by his mother. That face is Mathilde's—in Jungian terms, his *anima*, an archetype of the unconscious psyche that represents the opposite pole of the self, the non-self, either feminine or masculine (1976: 36-7; 42). For this reason, we cannot yet fully elaborate on the themes of love and alchemy; Mathilde has only appeared in dreams. However, we suspect that the realization of this blue flower will occur through love with Mathilde. For Novalis, love is the great alchemical work and the spiritual and aesthetic dimension of Romanticism.

In the conversation with his father, referring to having dreamed a lot during the night, it is interesting to note that, on one hand, his father states that dreams are "Schäume" (1945: 131), which can be translated as "foam" or "scum", both of which are valid here, either as something fragile and dissipating or as something vile. On the other hand, he says, "the times are no longer when divine visions accompanied dreams. [...] Back then, dreams must have had a different quality, just as with human things" (131-2),[25] invoking that primitive time already

---

[24] "die gegenseitige Durchdringung von Ich und Natur".

[25] "Die Zeiten sind nicht mehr, wo zu den Träumen göttliche Gesichte sich gesellten. [...] Damals muss es eine andere Beschaffenheit mit den Träumen gehabt haben, so wie mit den menschlichen Dingen".

discussed, a time of unity with nature, with things, and with the gods. These are two distinct positions concerning the chiliastic, millenarian belief that was quite popular in pietist circles. The son holds hope for the return of the golden age, while the father is sceptical of this dream. The latter shows disillusionment, diagnosing human fall, the decline of dreams, and the movement from revelation to dross.

According to Gnostic tradition, the fall gave rise to the separation of the sexes, splitting the hermaphrodite into two. It is thus important to consider how Heinrich will unleash his creative potential, affecting the world around him and creating the image of primordial unity. Ultimately, it will be shown that Heinrich's dream is not foam, but a transformative force; he is the realization Novalis sought, the messiah of nature equivalent to the coming of Christ to fulfil the millenarian dream. Ultimately, this is a return to the hermaphroditic one, which we have yet to address.

The fact that his father asserts that only the ancient and sacred scriptures can bring this supernatural [*überirdisch*] knowledge of the world suggests that Heinrich's dream is a source of access to this same knowledge, especially because, in his nested dream (the dream within the dream), he is beside the spring, and near it is the blue flower, the *flos sapientae*, the flower of wisdom. There are numerous indications of this coming messiah, which Heinrich himself understands. He responds by saying, "in the wisest books, one finds countless dream stories" (132),[26] confirming that these are of a subtle nature that brings reflections and that "the most confused dream, a peculiar apparition, [...] a significant tear in the mysterious curtain" (132).[27] Both in sacred scriptures and in alchemical treatises, these records of dreams, visions, and initiatory and revelatory deliriums appear. It is enough to lift the veil of the Hindu goddess Maya to reveal the illusory nature of reality.

If discovering the Stone is discovering eternity, then in Novalisian thought, the poet is the one who finds this eternal time, and he is the true alchemist, a revealer. For this reason, Novalis establishes a strong

[26] "in den weisesten Büchern findet man unzählige Traumgeschichten".
[27] "der verworrenste Traum, eine sonderliche Erscheinung, [...] ein bedeutsamer Riss in den geheimnisvollen Vorhang".

connection between poetry and dreams. Dreams unveil this eternal time, and poetry materializes it through words. Marcel Camus, in the preface to his French translation of *Ofterdingen*, asserts that dreams convey the will for infinity and that their wisdom is truer than that limited by common sense, external to the dream (1942: 33). Novalis also writes in *Das allgemeine Brouillon* that "dreams have greatly contributed to the culture and education of humanity" (1946b: 99).[28] In this sense, Heinrich concludes that dreams are "a friendly companion on the pilgrimage to the Holy Sepulchre" (1945: 133).[29] The Holy Sepulchre, where Christ resurrected, is the beginning of eternity; it is the symbol that unites Christ, the Stone, and, in Novalis, the dream and poetry. It is relevant to note that in the preparatory notes for *Ofterdingen*, Novalis writes that Jesus could be the hero of the work, with his homeland being that of the Holy Sepulchre (403). Novalis also mentions Jacob Böhme, who would appear at the end of the book (330), emphasizing his importance for composing the equivalence between Christ, the Stone, and Heinrich.

The image of the dream as a gear in the soul, like a great wheel propelling it forward (133) with a powerful impulse, might have been influenced by Böhme, who refers to divinity as a wheel. For Böhme, the wheel signifies the quality that gears the corporeal being of divinity (2013: 398). According to Böhme, God is the wheel of nature (656). In Heinrich's case, the dream possesses this divine quality that modifies, pulls, and pushes nature, which here can be equated with the soul. The debate between father and son about dreams is not yet concluded. It is pertinent to bring into the discussion Heinrich's father's dream, as it shares similar initiatory characteristics with his son's dream. Still in the waking world, but perhaps not fully awake, the father walks through the forest until he finds the house of an old man who offers him wine and shelter for the night, and shows him his books and antiquities, even reading poems to him. His host lived in a "heidnische Zeit" (1945: 135), a "pagan time", a time that was not his

---

[28] "die Träume haben sehr viel zur Kultur und Bildung der Menschheit beigetragen".

[29] "einen freundlichen Begleiter auf der Wallfahrt zum Heiligen Grabe".

own, celebrating the ancient world constituted by various arts.

The temporal aspect is important because it also bears an alchemical mark, associated with Saturn. At play is what Novalis calls "geistige Gegenwart", a spiritual or mental present, as he reveals, which identifies crystallization, the alchemical coagula phase, through dissolution, the alchemical *solve*. This present that crystallizes in dissolution diagnoses the atmosphere of the poet (1945b: 37). It also concerns the eternal present and the ouroboric eternal return, whose alchemical function is to dissolve and crystallize. Aby Warburg linked the temporal aspect of the ouroboros with the image of Cronos-Saturn, a deity who dissolves, destroys, liberates, and renews, as ruler of time (Bender *et al.* 2007: 210). He is sovereign of the golden age, appearing in alchemical treatises as alchemical *prima materia* (Roob 2006: 547), referring to the ouroboros egg. Time is understood as a primordial, titanic matter. Saturn, as the ruler of the process of destruction and renewal, is also considered the patron of alchemists (171). The process starts with Saturn-lead and progresses towards Sun-gold, i.e., towards the centre. It seems, for now, that the blue flower represents the liberation from the chains of time, allowing one to always be in the present, carrying the golden age within.

That night, Heinrich's father falls asleep and dreams that he leaves his home town to resolve something, feeling as joyful as if he were going to his wedding. This comparison is indeed reminiscent of Christian Rosenkreutz, who leaves his home after receiving an invitation to the royal wedding. Heinrich's father walks through meadows and finds himself at the foot of a mountain, within which there is a staircase. Upon seeing this staircase, he remembers his old host and feels as if he had been there in a very distant past, the same "heidnische Zeit" he had mentioned, reinforcing the idea of eternal return. He descends the staircase, discovers a well-lit cave, where an old man in a long robe sits at an iron table contemplating a beautiful young woman sculpted in marble. This episode also resembles the story of Rosenkreutz: already in the palace, Rosenkreutz is guided to a luminous room, illuminated by carbuncles, where he finds the sepulchre of Venus, with the goddess naked (1973: 98).

The hermit takes Heinrich's father's hand and leads him through various corridors until they reach a green meadow, full of lush trees, various flowers, and fountains. The father recalls that one particular flower caught his attention and, subsequently, he finds himself back at the top of the mountain with his guide, who says to him:

> You have seen the wonder of the world. You stand before the happiest being on earth and have the potential to become a renowned man. Take careful note of what I tell you: If you return here on St. John's Day towards evening and earnestly pray to God for the understanding of this dream, you will attain the highest earthly fortune; then, pay attention to a little blue flower that you will find up here, pick it, and humbly submit yourself to divine guidance. (1945: 137)[30]

After this episode, still dreaming, Heinrich's father finds himself surrounded by the most illustrious people of humanity, and the sound of their words turns into music. Suddenly, everything becomes dark, and Heinrich's mother appears with the baby Heinrich, radiating light. The baby grows, rises into the air, gains white wings, and lifts his parents with him, flying high until the earth appears like "a golden bowl with the cleanest carvings" (138).[31] Heinrich's father sees the flower, the old man, and the mountain once more and wakes up, filled with a violent passion for his future wife.

The father's dream possesses various hermeneutic keys from the hermetic tradition that deserve discussion. The notion of the golden age in the hermit's house, where poetry and art in general are the dominant crafts, is evident, as well as the theme of initiation: the use of the mountain, the staircase, and the cave all demonstrate this.

---

[30] "Du hast das Wunder der Welt gesehn. Es steht bei dir, das glücklichste Wesen auf der Welt und noch über das ein berühmter Mann zu werden. Nimm wohl in acht, was ich dir sage: Wenn du am Tage Johannis gegen Abend wieder hieher kommst und Gott herzlich um das Verständnis dieses Traumes bittest, so wird dir das höchste irdische Los zuteilwerden; dann gib nur acht auf ein blaues Blümchen, das du hier oben finden wirst, brich es ab, und überlass dich dann demütig der himmlischen Führung."

[31] "eine goldene Schüssel mit dem saubersten Schnitzwerk".

Furthermore, the hermit-guide sculpting the woman from marble, invoking Pygmalion and Galatea, and naturally, Ovid's *Metamorphoses*, also introduces the initiation to love through art. Sculpting and giving life to love; creating by transforming and manipulating matter.

The transformation of the sound of their words into music elevates and universalizes their language, allowing all the illustrious people of humanity to understand it. Music is related to the hermetic tradition, as Hermes invented and offered the lyre to Apollo, and regarding Pythagoras's theory of the harmony of the spheres, Johannes Kepler attributes the same idea to this god. Harmony and number compose the universe in the Pythagorean conception, with the micro and macrocosm connected by different tones and their heights (Roob 2006: 84). In this sense, the universe is interconnected by the mathematical and harmonic structure of sound, as alchemy believes in the correspondence between the micro and macrocosm. Heinrich's father's desire would be to achieve this harmony and wisdom in his speech, uniting all philosophical understandings of the world.

Böhme also considers sound as one of the seven forces that compose God, as previously discussed. The third, earthly sound, and the sixth, celestial sound, are related to Mercury, as Böhme clarifies: "Mercury or sound / Just like in the saltpetre of the earth / is the sound / from which grows gold, silver, copper, iron" (2013: 174).[32] Saltpetre is derived from dew and used for the philosophical fire that opens, grows, metals, and is sometimes identified with Mercury and the dragon (Roob 2006: 37). Therefore, the discourse transforms into music in its capacity for transmutation and improvement of matter. It is from the sound of his words, made into music, that universal understanding emerges. This process also evokes a return to an original time, as Novalis understands that our language was initially more musical and should become so again (1946: 267).

In his dream, the most significant aspect is the winged baby Heinrich, lifting his parents until they observe the earth as a golden bowl (a bowl that will become important in the future). This image

---

[32] "der Mercurius oder der Schall / Gleich wie in dem Salitter der Erden / ist der Schall / davon wechst Gold / Silber / kupffer / Eisen".

connects with the alchemical pair—sun and moon, sulphur and mercury, king and queen—in their conjunction, giving birth to the Philosopher's Stone. Thomas Vaughan's treatise, *Lumen de Lumine*, presents a man wandering in darkness—just as everything turned dark around Heinrich's father—until he finds the light of nature, Heinrich's mother, containing alkali salt, or the Arabic *Halicali*, pure and luminous like a child, who will discover the green dragon, the treasure or philosophical mercury (1919: 268).

The winged Heinrich recalls Hermes, the volatile mercury, and will also be significant for the character Eros later. It is revealed that he is the offspring of an alchemical conjunction; this is significant because it will be revealed later that Heinrich's father once possessed the purity of his own son. It is not yet about perfection or the hermaphrodite but rather about the seed with that potential. Thus, it is understood that there are no longer qualities in the dream for the father, as he has fulfilled his role in the alchemical equation, passing the next step to his son. Heinrich, as the product of fixed mercury and volatilized sulphur, will be the hermaphrodite, which at this point can be termed *Rebis*—a dual matter that, when unified, becomes the Philosopher's Stone (Paracelsus 1896: 396).

While the first chapter of *Ofterdingen* can be marked by the theme of the dream, the second chapter effectively begins the journey. This journey, as initiation, discovery, and conscious learning—since the dream developed them in the unconscious—represents Heinrich's entry into the circuit of trials that will lead him to return to the primordial one, the Adamic hermaphrodite. The unity achieved in Heinrich is the very origin of the hermaphroditic consciousness of the human being. The hermetic androgyne results from the reconciliation of polarities, and its myth "is at the centre of the speculations of the romantics, followers of Böhme. It is the active force that reintroduces eternity into time" (Centeno 1987: 80).[33] Thus, with the hermaphrodite, Rebis, the gathered matter, are related the conceptions of the golden age and the millenarian promise.

[33] "está no centro das especulações dos românticos, seguidores de Böhme. É a força actuante que permite reintroduzir a eternidade no tempo".

Heinrich's mother decides to travel to her home town, Augsburg, where his father lives, so that he can meet his grandson and, above all, because she notices that Heinrich has become more introspective [*stiller*], reserved [*in sich gekehrter*], even irritable [*missmütig*] and unwell [*krank*]. This state reflects Heinrich's adolescent phase, in which the need for transformation of the still-putrefying matter is evident. The debilitated state quickly ends upon learning of the journey, as he had always considered, from the accounts he had heard, that Augsburg was an "irdisches Paradies" (1945: 139), an "earthly paradise".

His departure was marked by his godmother gifting him a gold necklace. This object also appears around the neck of a unicorn that will be divided into two parts by a lion with a sword in *Chymische Hochzeit* (1973: 76), representing the separation of the fixed from the volatile, with the unicorn also possibly symbolizing mercury. The gold necklace itself, in Kircheweger's view in *Aurea Catena Homeri*, signifies that "one thing changes into another and through the everlasting alternation of things turns again into the same it had been before, or something similar" (2016: 74). Moreover, the necklace "connects within itself" (9), symbolizing the ouroboros entwined around the hermetic child, representing transformations and the eternal return. This is because Heinrich will return to his home town, but transformed. Therefore, this gift reminds him of the necessary union with the whole.

As Heinrich distances himself, he becomes melancholic, confronted with the awareness of separation, feeling that "infinite is the youthful sorrow at this first experience of the transience of earthly things, which is so necessary and indispensable for the inexperienced mind. [...] The first announcement of death, the first separation remains unforgettable" (141).[34] What the twenty-year-old experiences signifies the beginning of the alchemical operation in *prima materia*, in its *nigredo*. The bath in the golden basin is a foreshadowing of what

---

[34] "unendlich ist die jugendliche Trauer bei dieser ersten Erfahrung der Vergänglichkeit der irdischen Dinge, die dem unerfahrnen Gemüt so notwendig und unentbehrlich. [...] Eine erste Ankündigung des Todes, bleibt die erste Trennung unvergesslich".

may come, but it is not yet its realization. It is in this sadness, separation, *separatio*, and death, *putrefactio*, i.e., in the *solve* of the first phase of the hermetic operation, that he finds himself. Specifically, Heinrich separates from what was fixed to him and becomes volatile.

As the narrator indicates, this separation, when it becomes less distressing, as a "nächtliches Gesicht" (141), a "nocturnal vision", will turn into a "friendly guide and a comforting acquaintance" (141).[35] A part of what represents the fixed element for Heinrich will accompany him, namely his mother will join him on the journey: "the presence of his mother greatly comforted the young man" (141).[36] The use of the same verb "trösten" [to comfort] reinforces the maternal presence as initially being a comforting guide, a role that will be surpassed as Heinrich progresses in his journey, particularly in Augsburg. The fixed element is revealed by the phrase: "the old world seemed not yet completely lost" (141-2).[37] The ancient time, golden age, and origin are currently embodied in the figure of the mother. She may represent the image of the earth, a fixed element, which nurtures and supports the *filius philosophorum*, as shown in Michael Mayer's second emblem in *Atalanta Fugiens* (2007: 83), a woman whose womb is the terrestrial globe, nursing her child: "it is the Earth that feeds with its milk the child of the wise; only one who has the globe itself as its nurse can aspire to greatness" (Centeno 1983: 74).[38] In this case, the journey is also the globe itself, and since the destination is the maternal land, the mother had to accompany him.

The journey begins at the dawn of the day, and as the sun rises, Heinrich's dark thoughts transform into ancient melodies. He finds himself in a limbo where, in front of him, the blue flower unfolds, and behind him is the land of his birth, a past to which he knows he will return "and as if he were journeying back to it" (1945: 142).[39] This feeling confirms the presence of longing/ desiderium [*Sehnsucht*] in the symbolism of the blue flower and reinforces the movement of returning

---

[35] "freundlicher Wegweiser und eine tröstende Bekanntschaft".
[36] "die Nähe seiner Mutter tröstete den Jüngling sehr".
[37] "die alte Welt schien noch nicht ganz verloren".
[38] "é a Terra, que alimenta com o seu leite o filho dos sábios; só pode aspirar a ser grande aquele que tem por ama o próprio globo terrestre".
[39] "und als reise er daher diesem eigentlich zu".

to the primitive self. *Sehnsucht* indeed has a dual temporal movement: future, as longing, and past, as nostalgia. In *Ofterdingen* and Novalis's thought, these two times merge into *Sehnsucht*, exalting the previously invoked *geistige Gegenwart*. Heinrich moves towards a future to return to a past, which, in truth, expands the present, making it eternal.

The homeland, to which he yearns to return, belongs to that primordial time Heinrich initially mentioned,[40] when all things were interconnected in unity. Therefore, he feels that the steps he takes on this journey are steps of return, a path inward, towards the necessary learning to recover that golden age, that is, to complete the journey outward. The return to unity aligns with how Georg Welling addresses the issue of transmutation into gold in *Opus Mago-Cabbalisticum et Theosophicum*. Gold is the sun, and transmuting everything into the sun and making everything return to the origin is to recognize "nature in God and God in nature" (2006: xv): the transcendent immanent.

The emphasis on individual experience, the opportunity to undergo personal transformations and relate them to one's beliefs, is prominent in alchemical thought, as embraced by Pietism. Artistic creation, in this case poetic, reflects this process and allows for the expression of such a relationship, in line with Novalis's ideas. This approach underscores the differing ways in which the self is experienced. In this sense, one of the merchants travelling with Heinrich advises him not to neglect the pleasures of life, highlighting the misfortune of relying solely on individuals detached from their times and lacking experience.

Heinrich agrees with the merchant, although not entirely. According to the young man, direct experience is a laborious and lengthy path, whereas inner contemplation is "fast ein Sprung" (1945: 146), "almost a leap", as the former only reaches knowledge after exploring each observed experience individually, often without appreciating the broader context. In contrast, the latter path is characterized by "kindliche unbefangene Einfalt" (146), "childlike innocent simplicity" (146). Heinrich's expression, along with his impression that what he speaks of "kindische Träume" (146), "childish dreams", aligns with the

---

[40] Even though they are symptoms of interest in the Indo-European origins of language and the idea of an Eastern homeland, as previously noted.

image of the pure child discovering the alchemical treasure, as described by Vaughan. In a way, Heinrich criticizes the acquisition of knowledge solely through observable experience—by separating and analysing everything, thus losing the dimension of the whole, the spirit. Knowledge gained with consideration of the whole not only recalls the concept of *anima mundi* but also evokes Schelling's term *Weltseele*, or world soul, which Novalis studied, as noted in his letter to Karoline Schlegel (1946c: 258), and furthermore aligns with the hermetic premise of the correspondence between microcosm and macrocosm.

For Heinrich, experiencing from within, *ab intra*, or the *Weg nach Innen* [path to the interior], is what enables the *Weg nach Aussen* [path to the exterior]. Heinrich demonstrates the reconciliation of perceptual experiences that alchemists have long advocated. This inner contemplation is the hallmark of poets, and thus the merchants recognize his vocation. Evidence of knowledge through inner contemplation is that Heinrich already shows himself to be a poet, even without fully understanding what it means to be one. The merchant knows nothing about inner contemplation, or knowledge *ab intra*, and thus refers to the practice of activity in the world. Indeed, the merchant observes that no element of Heinrich's poetry is copied from the external world, unlike music and painting (148), which supports Heinrich's inner contemplation. In any case, both reject the lack of experience and alienation, whether internal or external.

The fact that the merchant does not follow Heinrich's reasoning is centred on Heinrich's vocation as a poet, as indicated by the merchant. What Heinrich knows about poetry is that ancient poets enjoyed divine protection and spoke of "himmlische Weisheit" (147-8), "heavenly wisdom". This revelation-like aspect of poetry connects with the alchemical quest for divine wisdom, or Gnostic Sophia. The merchant conveys this vision of the poet as God's emissary by stating "that a special constellation is required when a poet is to come into the world" (148).[41] This constellation marks the superior condition of the poet, equivalent to the gold of the alchemists.

---

[41] "[…] dass eine besondere Gestirnung dazu gehort, wenn ein Dichter zur Welt kommen soll".

The journey continues with the merchant recounting stories of ancient poets and their deeds in the age of gold. When the merchant refers to Greek poets who animated the forests and gave them life with their instruments, it is impossible not to think of Orpheus and his ability to enchant stones and animals with his lyre, which was given to him by his father Apollo and is of Hermetic invention. Hermes, as previously mentioned, combines music and alchemy, and it is implied that poetry arises from this conjunction, because, as the merchant also says, this ancient gift of poets revived plants, transformed the power of waters, and moved stones (151): the alchemy of the word and creation. It is the merchant himself who inscribes the poet within the Hermetic tradition, as a true alchemist, saying that:

> They were said to have been both seers and priests, legislators and doctors, drawing down even higher beings through their magical art and instructing them in the mysteries of the future, revealing to them the balance and natural arrangement of all things, as well as the inner virtues and healing powers of numbers, plants, and all creatures. According to legend, it was only then that the various tones and peculiar sympathies and orders came into nature, whereas before everything had been wild, disorderly, and hostile. (151)[42]

Here, we see the dream of the father fully developed: the transformation of the sound of his words into music, before the most illustrious figures of the world. This role of the poet as a transmuter and creator, akin to a minor deity, mirrors the alchemist-demiurge, reflecting the very creation of the universe. This underscores the

[42] "Sie sollen zugleich Wahrsager und Priester, Gesetzgeber und Ärzte gewesen sein, indem selbst die höhern Wesen durch ihre zauberische Kunst herabgezogen worden sind und sie in den Geheimnissen der Zukunft unterrichtet, das Ebenmaß und die natürliche Einrichtung aller Dinge, auch die innern Tugenden und Heilkräfte der Zahlen, Gewächse und aller Kreaturen ihnen offenbart. Seitdem sollen, wie die Sage lautet, erst die mannigfaltigen Töne und die sonderbaren Sympathien und Ordnungen in die Natur gekommen sein, indem vorher alles wild, unordentlich und feindselig gewesen ist."

affinity between the alchemist and the poet, both being under the protection of Hermes. The citation echoes Greek cosmogony, Pythagoreanism, and all pre-Christian esotericism, including Gnostic Christianity. It represents chaos organized by the alchemical operation of the poet, who, through the word, perfects nature.

Indeed, the connection to Orpheus has also been confirmed concerning the golden age. Joachim Mähl highlights the Platonic conception of this golden era, which was later disseminated by the Stoics, as an opening to the Judaic-Christian pastoral symbolism. This symbolism features an original language that facilitates communication between people and animals, extracting deeper insights about the world. This conception is rooted in Orphism and is present in *Ofterdingen* (1994: 37), given the previously described abilities of the Thracian bard.

The relation to Shamanism also appears significant. For Mircea Eliade, the initiatory death resembles the shamanic ritual. Besides Orpheus's descent into the underworld to obtain the gift of prophecy, some argue that the roots of Orphism are planted in Shamanism. Although not Homeric in tradition (Uždavinys 2011: 56), it may trace back to Siberian shamanic traditions that interacted with Thrace, as noted by historian Eric Dodds (1997: 140-147). This connection leads to the symbolism of death, as shamanic spirit possession involves a journey to the underworld, a view supported by historian Jean-Pierre Vernant (1990: 112). The shaman, as Francis Cornford states, "in the role of psychopomp, guides his companions to their destination and returns alone" (Cornford 1975: 152).[43] It is also interesting to note the value of the verb "to transit" and the French verb "transir" [to die]. Heinrich's return will indeed be solitary. The shaman possesses hermetic and Orphic competencies in the transition between life and death, between exoteric and esoteric knowledge, and between humans and animals. As I will attempt to demonstrate, Heinrich inherits this hermetic-Orphic legacy.

Furthermore, Uerlings supports this association by concluding that *Ofterdingen* is considered a work that straddles the boundary between

---

[43] "na qualidade de psicopompo, anima os seus companheiros até ao seu destino e regressa só".

alchemical-mystical metaphors and Novalis's philosophical-poetic intentions, read as a "mystical initiation, Orphic initiation, and introduction to absolute knowledge" (1991: 402).[44] Uerlings interprets Heinrich's dreams as a preliminary initiation and the bath of light as a baptism, referring to Orphic tradition, though not exclusively. The erotic charge fixes this intellectual experience in the act of creation, in which the soul ascends through art, and the poet, as the ultimate representative, unites exoteric experience with esoteric, inverting the world of existence and leading it back to its origin (1991: 411-12).

Based on the image of the poet projected by the merchant, a series of stories are narrated, and unique encounters occur during their journey to Augsburg. I will attempt to evoke the most significant symbolic experiences that corroborate Heinrich's connection to alchemy and prepare him for the most important teachings and his amorous conjunction.

The first tale recounts the episode of a young poet, blessed with many riches and jewels from his work as a bard, who manages to persuade a ship and its crew to take him to a certain country. However, driven by greed, the crew throws the poet into the sea after his final song. On account of the beauty and emotion of his words, a sea monster rescues him, transporting him across the waters to an island. Soon after, the monster seeks vengeance for the bard by recovering the treasures from the bottom of the sea, as the crew had fought over them, causing the ship to sink. Heinrich learns the value of imagination and that true gold and the Philosopher's Stone are to be found within oneself. Hillman, regarding the significance of the colour blue in alchemy, observes: "alchemy begins before we enter the mine, the forge, or laboratory. It begins in the blue vault, the seas, in the mind's thinking in images, imagining ideationally, speculatively" (2008: 35). Later, there will be encounters with caves and mines, but first and foremost Heinrich learns that diving into the unconscious, represented by the sea, is the initial experience necessary for both alchemy and

[44] "mystische Einweihung, orphische Initiation und Einführung in absolutes Wissen".

poetry. The treasure corrupted by thieves, the *nigredo*, sinks into the sea, transforms, and is discovered by the poet himself, in the sense that the sea monster is a creation of his own, dwelling within him.

In the second story, there is a king whose lineage traces to the East. For this king, royalty is not defined by the crown but by "that full, overflowing sense of bliss" (169).[45] For Jung, the idea of fullness represents alchemical perfection. The crown, in alchemy, symbolizes this fullness, the real totality, rather than power or wealth (Jung 1990: 26). This totality is also related to the conjunction of opposites, the multiple that is one, as Böhme conceives the image of God (2013: 118). He who attains perfection, i.e., fullness, or God, having reconciled all oppositions, will be king. The Eastern lineage also signifies perfection, as Paracelsus asserts: "the fermentation is prepared for gold, and the oriental King is born, sitting in his seat, and powerful above all the princes of this world" (1976: 87).

The monarch has two passions: poetry and his daughter. The latter, dressed in white, crowns the poet who wins the courtly contests, and "her entire soul had become a delicate song, a simple expression of melancholy and longing [...]: thus she was regarded as the visible soul of that splendid art" (1945: 155-6).[46] Poetry and the princess are a single symbol; she manifests the aura of poetry, her soul being music and made visible through the poetry. Crowning the poet aligns with the king's belief that poets are the noblest of men (157). His daughter could marry only the noblest of the noble. The crowned poet is the one who embodies totality and reconciliation of opposites, which, in Novalis's conception, encompasses the path both inward and outward. Heinrich continues to learn the value of the poet: first, in the treasure that he himself represents, and now in his coronation.

In the story, the princess encounters a young man after diving into a dark forest, which will soon be described as golden, indicating the well-established colours of alchemical symbolism. The house of the young man and his old father is depicted with an atmosphere of sanctity

[45] "jenes volle, überfließende Gefühl der Glückseligkeit".
[46] "ihre ganze Seele war ein zartes Lied geworden, ein einfacher Ausdruck der Wehmut und Sehnsucht [...]: so hielt man sie für die sichtbare Seele jener herrlichen Kunst".

[*Heiligkeit*] (159), an environment conducive to transmutation. During their farewell, the princess loses a ruby [*Karfunkel*], given by her mother, which has the power to grant freedom to its possessor, preventing them from being subjugated by anyone. In their second meeting, the young man returns it to her, but the girl offers it to him along with a gold necklace. The ruby, red and magical, whose German term also denotes "carbuncle", echoes the Philosopher's Stone, which, on a golden thread, encapsulates the meaning recently observed. Kirchweger, in *Aurea Catena Homeri*, promises that this carbuncle represents the union of the sun and the moon (2016: 255). Thus, the young man initiates the girl into the secrets of nature, and she teaches him about singing, poetry, and the lute. As described earlier, Rosenkreutz is also guided by carbuncles to the tomb of Venus.

One night, during a storm, they take refuge in a mossy and damp grotto, surrounded by almond tree branches and their fruits, and a spring of water. With the music of the lute and "wedding torches of lightning in the sweetest intoxication" (167),[47] they surrender to the transformation that the conjunction of their bodies allows. The next day, the princess reveals her royal lineage, the young man decides to ask for her hand in marriage from the king, and the old father shelters the princess in the underground chambers of his house, as she has become pregnant. After a year of great sorrow at the royal court, the young man appears, singing about the origins of the world from an ancient oak, heralding the return of the golden age with the supreme deities, Love and Poetry, to reign. In his final poem, the young man concludes: "to glory upon a throne / the poet ascends rough steps / and becomes the king's son" (173).[48] As he sings the last verse, the old man appears with the princess and "ein wunderschönes Kind" (147), "a beautiful child". The king's favourite eagle hovers above them with a golden diadem in its beak, which it places on the young man's head, who then immediately places it on the child's head. Everything ends well in the legendary Atlantis, the only mention of the location,

[47] "Hochzeitsfackeln der Blitze in den süßesten Rausch".
[48] "zur Glorie um einen Thron / der Dichter steigt auf Rauen Stufen / hinan und wird des Königs Sohn".

reinforcing the still fantastic and distant nature of this reality.

This tale could be explored in much greater depth than is presented here. What is essential to highlight is the learning that resonates with Heinrich. The real conjunction is present, a conjunction that has passed through the *nigredo* of the dark forest and stormy night, which is purified (*albedo*) in the mutual development of the young couple, through poetry, music, and natural sciences. The golden daylight and the gold necklace, along with the reddish carbuncle, evoke the awakening of love between them, and the mossy and damp grotto, with almond tree branches and a spring of water, is the ideal location for their conjunction, symbolizing fertility. Regarding the almond tree, Basil Valentine notes in *The Last Will* that almond wood and fruit shells are the best materials for burning and working with metals (2016: 57). Hence, their love consummates and transforms them, under the ideal conditions for the process.

The second, perfect conjunction occurs with the coronation of the young couple, the king's blessing, and the fruit, the child, which relates to Heinrich's father's dream in which the son appears as "ein glänzendes Kind" (1945: 138), "a radiant child". The interconnection between dreams, tales, and experiences, as well as the dissolution of time and space, will recur throughout *Ofterdingen*. As Mähl points out, the relationship between the children is "a hint towards Heinrich's calling as a poet and his messianic mission of salvation" (1994: 368).[49] The oak tree from which they emerge can be interpreted in various ways, one of which relates to the feminine and maternity, as noted by Jung (1990: 104), and this interpretation is significant given that the princess is motherless and there is no mention of the young man's mother. For the perfect conjunction to occur, the queen, i.e., the mother, the feminine element, must be present. The eagle symbolizes volatile mercury (Roob 2006: 288). In *Aurora Consurgens* by Thomas Aquinas, the eagle represents the south wind, which unites opposites to form the hermaphrodite (376), thus explaining why the diadem is carried by it.

---

[49] "ein Hinweis auf Heinrichs Berufung zum Dichter und seinen messianischen Erlösungsauftrag".

The tale serves as a prophecy for the coming of Mathilde, Heinrich's future beloved, and her father, Klingsohr, the master poet. Heinrich receives from this tale confirmation that love and poetry must go hand in hand, and indeed, several parallels with his future can be drawn when his vocation is fulfilled. Concurrently, he receives the sung words of the young man, learning about the chiliastic theme of the golden age. For now, it is sufficient to note that these tales and this journey constitute a second initiation for the young poet. Heinrich is gradually preparing, at a gentle heat, as the alchemists prescribe.

At this point in the journey, the stories cease, and Heinrich experiences two different situations. In one stop, Heinrich and his mother are welcomed at a castle, where the baron, their host and a former knight, dines with other knights. They exalt the Holy Land and the Holy Sepulchre, announcing preparations for a new Crusade, to which all of Europe will be summoned by the call of the Cross to Jerusalem, to fight the infidels of the East. The sword and the cross are united in the baron's words and the Crusader hymn sung by the knights, causing distress in Heinrich and leading him to imagine the Holy Sepulchre as a pale and noble young man, sitting on a stone, mistreated and gazing at a cross (1945: 181-82). This medieval imagery, vividly deployed here, teaches Heinrich about war under the banner of Christendom. From the description of the Holy Sepulchre, we see that Novalis disapproves of the cruelty of the Crusades. The homeland of Christ is contested between the West and the East, and the path marked by war contrasts with Heinrich's path, which, as he initially stated, would be shaped by the company of dreams. The path proposed by the West is not the path for the young poet.

Upon leaving the castle, Heinrich hears a female voice singing a sad song accompanied by a lute, lamenting the past, the motherland, and youth. When he finds her, desolate, with a child by her side, she finds his face reminiscent of her brother, who had left for Persia to visit a renowned poet who also played the lute. This constant presence of poetry and the figure of the poet, as well as music, particularly the lute, and Eastern lands, highlights the original musicality of language.

Zulima, the woman, recalls the power of Arabian poetry to capture the charms and mysteries of Nature, describing the fertile landscapes of her homeland, Edenic reminiscences typical of Romantic landscapes, as Johann Adelung adumbrated them in his German dictionary, "excellently pleasant and equally enchanting regions" (1798: 1155).[50] She speaks about her ancient writing, inscribed on millennia-old stones, and how this writing leads to self-knowledge by recovering another world, in which the universe transforms into "magical poetry and fable of our senses" (187),[51] reminiscing about Novalis's thoughts on Sanskrit. The recurring theme is the return to a fertile nature and the transformative power of poetry. We should also not forget the word "Fabel", Fabula, fable, which is central in Klingsohr's tale. The similarity between Heinrich and Zulima's brother endows our protagonist with a mythically Eastern origin, the origin of all poets.

Soon after delving into the mysteries of Arabian poetry, Zulima presents herself as a counterpoint to the opinion of the knights at the castle, assuring Heinrich that her compatriots are not as violent or cruel as the knights profess. She also asserts that a visit to the Holy Sepulchre could have been accomplished without the strife that forever divided Europe and the East, and that "how beautiful would have been its holy grave as the cradle of a happy understanding, the occasion for eternal benevolent alliances" (188).[52] This message not only comes from Zulima but echoes again Novalis's sentiments in *Die Christenheit oder Europa*, where he writes in agreement with Zulima: "only patience, it will, it must come, the holy time of eternal peace, when the new Jerusalem will be the capital of the world" (1946c: 34).[53] Heinrich's education is holistic. He develops not only lyrical initiation and sensitivity to the marvellous tale but also a comprehensive understanding of the world around him.

At the last stop before Augsburg, there is an old foreigner who seeks treasures within the mountains. His quest began when a traveller

---

[50] "vorzüglich angenehmen und gleichsam bezaubernden Gegenden".
[51] "zauberische Dichtung und Fabel unserer Sinne".
[52] "und wie schön hätte sein heiliges Grab die Wiege eines glücklichen Einverständnisses, der Anlass ewiger wohltätiger Bündnisse werden können".
[53] "nur Geduld, sie wird, sie muß kommen die heilige Zeit des ewigen Friedens, wo das neue Jerusalem die Hauptstadt der Welt seyn wird".

encouraged him to become a miner. The old foreigner found a master who initiated him, and he owed all his knowledge to this master. The first time he encountered gold, "König der Metalle" (1945: 95), "King of Metals", he viewed it as a prisoner that needed to be freed to be honoured with crowns, chalices, and relics, and, through coins, to lead and dominate the world. When the old man was initiated, he was promoted to a miner [*Häuer*], one who actually works the rock, quarrying it to extract what lies within. Through his vocation, he also discovered love for his master's daughter, and on the day of his engagement, he found a vein of gold that earned him great praise and allowed him to give a golden necklace to his bride: the transmutation of gold, of himself, which led him to union with his partner. An outsider, encouraged by another outsider, now encourages Heinrich towards his final initiation before meeting Klingsohr, the master who will also lead him to the love of his daughter. The heart of the mountains and the caves, initiation, and the unconscious. As Hillman reminds us: first, there is the plunge into the blue of the ocean, and then entering the mine and its laboratory.

The miner "retains the childlike mood in which everything appears to him with its own peculiar spirit and in its original colourful wonder" (199),[54] and learns to work with "unermüdliche Geduld" (200), "tireless patience". His reflection on the vocation of mining leads him to conclude that "it must have been a divine man who first taught humans the noble art of mining and hid this serious symbol of human life in the bosom of the rocks" (201),[55] which he reveals to be the cross. Here we see the connection between the poet and the alchemist. The childlike disposition, already noted in Heinrich, seems to be a *sine qua non* for working with the material of the human spirit and nature, and for extracting what is primordial in the world. Indeed, the benefits of gold and the Philosopher's Stone lie in this immortality and youthful

---

[54] "behält die kindliche Stimmung, in der ihm alles mit seinem eigentümlichsten Geiste und in seiner ursprünglichen bunten Wunderbarkeit erscheint".

[55] "Das muss ein göttlicher Mann gewesen sein, der den Menschen zuerst die edle Kunst des Bergbaus gelehrt und in dem Schoße der Felsen dieses ernste Sinnbild des menschlichen Lebens verborgen hat".

spirit and body. Patience is intrinsic to the arduous work of transmutation; the "rough steps" that the young man had to ascend to become a king in the tale of the merchants exemplify this. The art of Vulcan is invoked here, with the epithet of "divine man", alongside Hermes and Vulcan, who teach these crafts. Paracelsus discusses an inner Vulcan, symbolizing the *athanor*, the alchemical furnace (2008: 588), also known as the *archeus*, the organ responsible for the separation and digestion in the alchemical process (15). Human perfectibility and its slow yet profound process are inscribed within the work of mining, alchemy, and poetry.

This cross is not derived solely from Christianity; it is much older and encompasses elements and qualities of the state of matter. The arduous work of the miner to uncover gold embodies the condition revealed by the cross, a symbol of the domination of matter, the four elements, the union of opposites, and ultimately, human life. This recalls a passage from Goethe's poem "Die Geheimnisse" (The Secrets or Mysteries):

[...] The cross stands closely embraced by roses.
Who has adorned the cross with roses?
The wreath swells, softly accompanying
The rugged wood from every side.
And light silver clouds of heaven float,
Soaring upwards with cross and roses,
And from the centre wells forth a sacred life
Threefold rays that emanate from a single point! (1829: 189)[56]

In its Rosicrucian essence, the poem, as Gray reflects, "represents for him [Goethe] the combination of stern wrath and tender love. Christ's

[56] "[...] Es steht das Kreuz mit Rosen dicht umschlungen.
Wer hat dem Kreuze Rosen zugesellt?
Es schwillt der Kranz, um recht von allen Seiten
Das schroffe Holz mit Weichheit zu begleiten.
Und leichte Silber-Himmelswolken schweben,
Mit Kreuz und Rosen sich emporzuschwingen,
Und aus der Mitte quillt ein heiliges Leben
Dreifacher Strahlen, die aus Einem Punkte dringen!"

death is a necessary part of his glorious resurrection" (2010: 200). The combination of wrath and love evokes Böhme: the cross and the rose, contraction and expansion, which create the universe. In this sense, the arduous work in the mine is compensated by the resurrection of the gold that longs for life, as the miner believes.

The miner asserts that song, poetry, the cithara, and dance are always present in his profession, once again emphasizing the direct relationship between alchemy, in the task of mining, and music: the visible and the invisible, the concrete and the abstract are transformed into each other. One of the old man's songs speaks of an intimate correspondence with this secret workshop [*geheimen Bau*], likening it to a bride (202). The grotto, the mine, as places of self-knowledge, represent the construction of the material world created by Sophia, the eternal bride of Christ and the primordial Adam. The sacred air of the mine belongs to an original, primitive world [*Vorwelt*], which allows a return to the golden age.

Another song sung outside was passed to the old man by another miner. This indecipherable poem, according to him, tells of a king who lives in a castle that emerged from the sea, who binds his subjects with an invisible thread that comes from his chest, without them knowing they are slaves. The king bathes in waters to purify his limbs, and his rays shine in the white blood of his mother. Only knowledge could destroy the people's imprisonment, and when this happens, the sea would flood the castle, and the people would return to their homeland. The king's emergence from the sea, from the unconscious, enabled him to dominate the people; he freed himself from his prison, attaining hermetic knowledge. The people must do the same to return to their origin. This origin, already vaguely professed, directed towards the golden age, the celestial homeland, God, and nature, may also correspond to the figure of the mother.

Firstly, as Gray asserts, "the male or active principle is [...] represented by the King, who is Gold, while the passive principle is represented by the Mother, or Mercury" (2010: 31). The king being gold is also being the sun, and thus the invisible threads that command the people, less pure metals-planets, become an effect of the sun's gravity that promotes translation. The white blood of the mother, mercurial water, or *luna philosophorum*, purifies and sublimates the gold which, as confirmed by Welling, is the very origin of God in nature and vice versa. Welling also states that "we treat Mercury in greater detail, as well as the true location of Paradise" (2006: 85). Gray cites verses from Welling that Goethe claimed to have read. Since they do not appear in Welling's *Opus Mago-Cabbalisticum Et Theosophicum*, they are quoted from Gray:

[…] we must come remoulded from the mother's body. /
For I cannot otherwise reach the Kingdom of Heaven /
Unless I am born a second time. /
Therefore my desire is to return to the mother's womb /
That I may be regenerated […]. /
To this end the mother herself has urged this King, /
And hastened to receive him with motherly love [...]. (2010: 32)

The maternal womb corresponds to the alchemical retort, and the bath will regenerate it back to its origin, which is also the *prima materia*, the very Philosopher's Stone. As Gray states, "it was useless to attempt the production of the Stone until the original Matter had been found, and that this in turn could not be discovered until the Stone had been made" (2010: 19). Gray further explains, drawing on Paracelsus's studies, that "who would enter the Kingdom of God must first enter with his body into his mother, and there die" (31). In Heinrich's first dream, he bathes in a basin of light within a grotto, and now, while awake, he enters the grotto as if emerging once again from the maternal womb.

Heinrich explores the grottoes with the miner, which show signs of being from ancient times, equivalent to the very maternal uterine origin. Upon hearing a song extolling love, describing it as a cup of drink that opens the gates of heaven, they encounter a man of indeterminate age. In the vast space of the grotto where he is found, there are several books, a lyre, and a full suit of armour, indicating that he was once a warrior. Thus, music, poetry, knowledge, and warfare represent the synthesis of everything Heinrich has learned in the previous chapters. On a stone table, there are life-size engravings of a man and a woman, holding a crown of lilies and roses, with an inscription that reads: "Friedrich and Marie von Hohenzollern: returned to their homeland" (216).[57]

We will later develop issues concerning this homeland, this couple, and the symbolism of the lilies and roses. The fact that they have returned here, to the grotto, to their homeland, evokes once again the maternal origin and the holy sepulchre, as signs of death and rebirth, initiation and conjunction. This subterranean space, with the woman buried there, belongs to the same order as the underworld, where Eurydice resides; the underworld as an initiation project, where death and life merge, transforming the novice into an alchemical adept. If, in Heinrich's father's dream, the earth is a golden cup, here love is a cup that, when drunk, opens the gates of heaven. To live on earth and experience love is to attain paradise and fulfilment in life. It is love that leads to divine knowledge, Sophia.

This man, who is ultimately Hohenzollern, discusses the importance of memory and asserts that only mature men, at the end of their personal history, should write about history. He also argues that a historian must be well-acquainted with all the details, grasp the essence of the facts, and be able to recount them in an engaging and instructive manner. On account of his unique talent for linking events, Hohenzollern considers that a historian must necessarily also be a poet. The poet perceives "with silent pleasure their delicate feeling for the mysterious spirit of life. There is more truth in their fairy tales than in learned chronicles" (219).[58]

Another idea highlighted by both Hohenzollern and the old miner is the organization of nature over time. According to them, nature began in a state of violence and chaos and gradually organized itself, achieving harmony and calm. On one hand, this led to a reduction in nature's fecundity and the exhaustion of creative force, evidenced by the absence of new metals, precious stones, mountains, animals, and plants. On the other hand, nature gained refinement, greater

---

[57] "Friedrich und Marie von Hohenzollern: kehrten auf dieser Stelle in ihr Vaterland zurück".

[58] "mit stillem Vergnügen ihr zartes Gefühl für den geheimnisvollen Geist des Lebens. Es ist mehr Wahrheit in ihren Märchen als in gelehrten Chroniken".

sensitivity, and increased diversity in imagination and symbolic production, becoming more akin to human artistry (223).

This transformation of nature from chaos to organization reflects an artistic gesture, aligning with the idea shared by the merchant with Heinrich, in which the poet organizes wild and chaotic nature. If nature reduces its fecundity by organizing chaos, and considering that the Romantic project always works with the chaos of matter, we can conclude that the task involves not only organizing nature but also liberating it. Thus, both the poet and the alchemist share the role of transmuting the real and organizing the cosmos. As noted by Schefer (2005: 30), chaos is the origin that, when organized, grants access to knowledge by extracting all the potentialities of life, similar to what is done in the alchemical laboratory.

One of the books caught Heinrich's attention. Written in Provençal, with various images related to knights and figures familiar to Heinrich, it reflects a medieval ideal. The detail that the book is in Provençal, which Heinrich finds difficult to understand, suggests that it might be a romance, as "Provençal verse and prose tales, mostly about knights and their chivalrous exploits, assumed the name 'romance'" (Schulz 2004: 26). In one of the illustrations, Heinrich recognizes his own likeness. He then identifies two other figures, the old miner and the hermit Hohenzollern. As he continues to leaf through the book, he finds other characters from his life depicted, including his parents, the court chaplain, and other familiar figures, all dressed in attire from different eras. At the end of the book, there is an image of Heinrich with a guitar in hand, embracing a beautiful young woman on the deck of a ship, fighting men with a wild appearance, or conversing amiably with Saracens and Moors. In other images, there is also an unknown man, but one who evokes happiness and reverence in Heinrich. We are aware that this unknown man is Klingsohr, and that the beautiful young woman is Mathilde. Finally, the last images in the book are incomprehensible to him, featuring figures similar to those in his dream (227-28).

Uerlings identifies in this book another sign of Orphic initiation, drawing from Eckhard Heftrich's study. He observes that the book itself symbolizes anamnesis, the creative rediscovery of the archetype, in which the future is already recounted as history, much like in inspired books of a transcendental time, such as sacred scriptures (1991: 412). Viewing one's history, recognizing it as past even if it is also one's future, engages with the Socratic-Platonic idea that learning is a form of recollection and the broader German concept of *Sehnsucht* observed earlier. Past and future, nostalgia and yearning, highlight the eternal return or ouroboric cycle, the *geistige Gegenwart*, the spiritual present. As Schefer comments, "the quest for a centre of the earth magically leads to the heart of literature [...], which is irresistibly evoked by the 'book' consulted by Henri" (2005: 95).[59] The centre of the earth, when reached, expands consciousness to be contemporaneous with the moment of world creation. Mähl further notes that in this process of learning through recollection, the episode of Aeneas's shield is evoked (1994: 93). At play is the idea of fate: the prophecy made, lived, and relived always by the protagonist, destined for great deeds.

Before resuming the action, the narrator discusses the difference between heroes and poets. Broadly speaking, heroes place their souls at the service of their intellect, acting as its servants. Their lives consist of a series of events, as heroes are born for action and not for contemplation. In contrast, poets possess souls that encompass the universe, and their sole activity is to contemplate, seeking to capture the aforementioned *Weltseele*, the spiritual unity of all things. This spirit enables them to play the mysterious role of the soul. They have feet of gold, and their presence gives wings to humans. Through their sensitivity, they discover the essence of the world within themselves. Because of this, only they have the full right to be called wise. Poetry awakens the hero, not the other way around. Heinrich is one of these rare, winged poets, though his soul, or speech [*das Gespräch*], has not yet awakened.

The hero can be associated with the initial state of *prima materia*, which needs to be purified through fire (*calcinatio*); one who experiences the actions of transmutation but does not recreate himself,

[59] "la quête d'un centre de la terre conduit magiquement au coeur de la littérature [...], qu'évoque irrésistiblement le 'livre' consulté par Henri".

as his deeds will be recounted by others, the poets. He represents action, the struggle against impurity and internal chaos, striving to achieve perfection. The hero acts in the external world, performing deeds that symbolize the transformation of physical reality, such as the quest for the Philosopher's Stone or universal healing. In turn, the poet can be seen as one who enters the stage of *albedo*, where matter is dissolved into its spiritual essence. He contemplates and reflects the spirit of things, seeking inner enlightenment. The heroes of antiquity are often demigods or chosen ones who undertake epic journeys to restore order to the world. Poets or bards preserve and transmit these stories, serving as guardians of cultural and spiritual memory. The hero represents the quest of the ego to overcome challenges and grow, while the poet symbolizes the connection to the collective unconscious, bringing to light profound and universal truths.

Thus far, Heinrich has been on a path to receive his first alchemical guide, one who will lead him toward transmutation and conjunction.

2.3. SOUND, THE CONDUCTOR OF THE WORK

Heinrich and his mother arrive in Augsburg, and at the house of his grandfather, the old Schwaning, Heinrich immediately recognizes one of the men from the hermit Hohenzollern's book: the poet Klingsohr. Heinrich becomes so engrossed in the singularity of the event and the man that he does not notice a young woman, who is also very familiar. It is the grandfather who points her out—Mathilde, Klingsohr's daughter—and suggests the possibility of a romance between the two. Observing Heinrich's initial indifference, the grandfather remarks: "it is noticeable that you come from the North" (1945: 235),[60] and consequently, "in his homeland, spring comes late" (236).[61] This assertion may be of interest as it could relate to the later tale of Klingsohr. While Heinrich's interest in both Klingsohr and Mathilde is developed simultaneously, it is noteworthy that the first to arouse Heinrich's curiosity is the poet.

[60] "man merkt es, dass du aus Norden kommst".
[61] "in seinem Vaterlande kommt der Frühling spät".

The process of *ceratio* corresponds to the stage in alchemical work, following purification and removal of impurities, in which the solid metal must become fusible, able to merge with another substance (Holmyard 2012: 89-90). Heinrich and reality itself will undergo this process by means of Klingsohr's guidance,[62] learning to create and transmute nature. Klingsohr will meld the external world with the internal world, reality with imagination, through poetry and love.

Klingsohr diagnoses Heinrich as having a clear and expansive soul [*umfassend*], and Schwaning recommends him as his disciple. He also mentions the former inclination of Heinrich's father towards poetry, though now degenerated, confirming the transmission of the father's legacy to the son, in the realm of dreams and poetry. It is also significant that the mother, who encouraged the father to pass on his legacy to the son, is now replaced by the maternal grandfather, who guides Heinrich to the master and to love. Thus, Klingsohr is explicitly Heinrich's first initiatory guide. The nature of this learning process remains to be explored

In his first lesson, Klingsohr instructs Heinrich about the soul, nature, and poetry. He asserts that nature

> is to our soul what a body is to light. It holds it back; it refracts it into peculiar colours; it ignites a light on its surface or within its depths, which, if it equals its darkness, makes it clear and transparent, and if it exceeds it, emits light to illuminate other bodies. But even the darkest body can be made bright and shiny through water, fire, and air. (249)[63]

---

[62] The name of the poet Klingsohr clarifies his role: "klingen" [to sound] and "Ohr" [ear]. Thus, he represents the sound of poetry.

[63] " [...] ist für unser Gemüt, was ein Körper für das Licht ist. Er hält es zurück; er bricht es in eigentümliche Farben; er zündet auf seiner Oberfläche oder in seinem Innern ein Licht an, das, wenn es seiner Dunkelheit gleichkommt, ihn klar und durchsichtig macht, wenn es sie überwiegt, von ihm ausgeht, um andere Körper zu erleuchten. Aber selbst der dunkelste Körper kann durch Wasser, Feuer und Luft dahin gebracht werden, dass er hell und glänzend wird".

In this analogy nature retains the soul, refracting it into unique colours, igniting it with light, and, if it is dark—i.e., impure—nature, through the elements of water, fire, and air, makes it clear and bright. Nature thus plays the role of transforming the soul. The soul undergoes a series of colour changes, akin to the *cauda pavonis*, the peacock's tail, until it becomes a centre of light. Among the elements mentioned, earth is notably absent. This can be understood as the nurse from the *Tabula Smaragdina*, or the body itself, or the womb where transformations and life occur. Water is associated with the virtue of creation, fire also contributes to creation but is primarily responsible for sustaining it, and air, representing the animating breath or pneuma, drives transformation. In *Ofterdingen*, air is closely related to music and words. The constant presence of musical instruments and singing highlights the immaterial nature of air and music, paralleling Hermes, the winged messenger of words.

In this light, which the body must retain and contain, and which nature itself must instil in the soul to purify and perfect it, corresponds to Paracelsus's idea that the light of nature must be mastered by the physician, the alchemist, to distinguish the true from the false, the pure from the impure, and thus to heal. Paracelsus refers to this light of nature as the true alchemy (2008: 340). In Novalis's perspective, the light of nature, or alchemy, and the physician correspond to poetry and the poet, as he writes in *Fragmente des Jahres 1798*: "Poetry is the great art of constructing transcendental health. The poet is thus the transcendental doctor" (1946: 25).[64] The body-nature transmutes its own light, soul, through redemptive poetry. The soul, like light, is, for Klingsohr, elastic and permeable (1945: 251), meaning it is transmutable.

Regarding the perception of nature, Klingsohr taught Heinrich that it should be done through pleasure, soul and temperament [*Gemüt*], and intellect [*Verstand*]. According to the poet, soul and intellect usually oppose each other. The ideal would be to unite these two sources of perception so that the poet can understand nature through

---

[64] "Poesie ist die grosse Kunst der Konstruktion der transzendentalen Gesundheit. Der Poet ist also der transzendentale Arzt".

the combination of these opposites. This third path, the union of the inner and outer ways, is what Heinrich discussed with the merchant, and which Ralf Liedtke sees as the union of creativity with natural sciences, poetizing science (2003: 97-130).

Klingsohr explains that poetry only manifests itself in the presence of a poet and that Heinrich's journey had been narrated through accounts of poets for this reason. The merchants acted as voices of his genius, as his heralds: "your companions have unnoticed become his voices" (254).[65] The voice and movement of the journey connect with air, the wind that carries the *filius philosophorum* in its womb. Heinrich travels over water and with his mother, with water and earth accompanying him. As the *Tabula Smaragdina* states: "the Wind carried him in its womb and the Earth is its nurse" (Roob 2006: 9).[66]

The fire that must cook the material is, in Klingsohr's view, gaining substance. The processes of cooking and digesting are reflected in the episode in which the master summarizes the lessons Heinrich has acquired from each adventure on his journey. From Zulima, in the land of poetry, in the romantic East [*Morgenland*], Heinrich learned the sweet melancholy; the tales of war revealed to him its wild magnificence, while Nature and History were presented through the miner and the hermit. Finally, Heinrich himself is reminded of the ultimate lesson: love. At this point, the young couple confirm their desire to be together, with Heinrich stating that their eternity would already be a result of Mathilde's work.

In this context, Klingsohr symbolically marries them, wishing them to love each other until death, believing that love and fidelity will make their lives a perpetual poetry. Here, the fire dissolves and reduces all the elements of the *prima materia* and also coagulates them, managing to fix the masculine and the feminine. Welling reduces salt, sulphur, and mercury to a single element: fire; he even says that water itself is, in reality, fire (2006: 32). If we understand Mathilde as the element of water, or mercurial water, she, being Klingsohr's daughter, would also be fire, as she is a fiery guide, symbolizing the catalytic nature and

[65] "eure Gefährten sind unbemerkt seine Stimmen geworden".
[66] "o Vento transportou-o no seu ventre e a Terra é a sua ama".

sulphur of the equation, including the spirit, and specifically, the spirit of poetry. As Paracelso asserts: "in the fire of Sulphur is a great tincture for gems, which, indeed, exalts them to a loftier degree than Nature by herself could do" (1976: 27).

Heinrich can be seen as salt, the body, which "must be bathed, washed and purified" (Welling 2006: 38), considering the dream of bathing in light, the presence of water throughout his journey, and his entire initiation process. Thus, he must also be considered as fire, from Welling's perspective and possibly Novalis's, given that Heinrich and Klingsohr share the same calling, the vocation of poets. What has yet to happen is the ignition of Heinrich's fire, or at least outside of the dream. The unconscious content, the poet's vocation, needs to be faced and developed, meaning that poetry must be integrated into his consciousness and personality. Klingsohr opens the way for Mathilde, the poetry in love, to enter Heinrich's life.

In their reflections, both master and disciple, the poets Klingsohr and Heinrich, discuss war from a poetic perspective. They agree that war can be viewed as a poetic work in which the primordial waters [*Urgewässer*] contribute to the creation of new lands and peoples. For Klingsohr, the true war is the war of religion, where "the madness of men appears in its complete form" (1945: 256).[67] Through this madness, the war hero can be equated with an authentic poet, becoming a cosmic force [*Weltkraft*] imbued with poetry. A poet who is also a hero will be a messenger of God, though risking the boundaries of human strength. Thus, chaos must appear in the poem through an organization of ideas. Both the poet and the war hero, and the love and anger of Böhme, shape primordial chaos, taking a demiurgical role in creation, just as the primordial creator did, within the tension of contraction and expansion forces.

The correspondence between the microcosm and the macrocosm can also be revisited in Heinrich's reflections. Language, described as a "small world in signs and sounds" (259),[68] i.e., a microcosm, relates to the greater world, the macrocosm. Heinrich believes that the more a

---

[67] "der Wahnsinn der Menschen erscheint in seiner völligen Gestalt".
[68] "kleine Welt in Zeichen und Tönen".

person masters the language, the more they will desire to dominate the world and express themselves freely. This pleasure in revealing the world underpins the primordial tendency of being and the origin of poetry. Complementing this pleasure, Klingsohr observes that poetry is a natural activity of the human spirit, as it is constantly imagining and creating something. Drawing on Schefer's interpretation, one can see that Novalis views "poetic language [as] a reflection of natural language upon itself" (2005: 24-5).[69] Poetry, a "symbole de totalité" (25), a "symbol of totality", is the universe's self-awareness, as Novalis thinks.

Klingsohr's final lesson is of a practical nature, reflecting the role of the artist as a demiurge, akin to a true alchemist. He assures Heinrich that the creation of a marvellous and symbolic tale, or *Märchen*, is rarely successful when attempted by a young poet.[70] However, Klingsohr proceeds to narrate a tale of his own, written during his youth. In recounting his *Märchen*, the effect will be an expansion of consciousness, a fusion of the inner world with the outer, and a blending of the transcendent with the immanent. This marks the final learning experience for Heinrich with his guide.

2.4. *MÄRCHEN*: A MODEL OF WORK

In the tale, elements of alchemy, Gnosticism, Kabbalah, and Christianity are interwoven into a mixture of philosophical textures that Novalis crafts in *Ofterdingen*. I will focus on the alchemical elements and some other relevant details to study the alchemical role of Klingsohr in Heinrich's life.

This *Märchen* encapsulates all the points developed thus far, drawing from symbolic traditions present in alchemy and Hermeticism. It demonstrates the potential fusion of the poetic with the mystical, the dream with the real, and alchemy with literature

---

[69] "le langage poétique [comme] une réflexion de la langue naturelle sur elle-même".

[70] Uerlings draws attention to points of comparison between the characters in Klingsohr and the characters in Goethe's *The Green Snake and the Beautiful Lily* (cf. 1991: 502).

within the Romantic project. Consequently, the ouroboric process is presented: from formless chaos to differentiation, leading to the unity of polarities through love and poetry, creating the image of the hermaphroditic hermetic, the *prima materia* that fabricates the Philosopher's Stone, i.e., the self in plenitude with nature, achieving the eternal present, the moment of creation. In examining the tale, I will focus on King Arthur and his daughter Freya, a heraldic bird, Eros and Fable, their parents, Ginnistan, the nurse of Eros and Fable, the divine Sophia, a scribe, a sleeping queen, King Luna, who is the father of Ginnistan, a sphinx, and Perseus.

Klingsohr's tale should not be viewed exclusively as an alchemical allegory. It represents a culmination and synthesis of ideas previously discussed, symbolically conveyed, and maximally enhancing creativity, always emphasizing the transformative dimension of reality. The kingdom in the tale is in crisis, with the challenge of returning to the golden age. One of the aspects already explored is the fact that the characters in the tale embody archetypes of the self (Molnár 1987: 117).

King Arthur introduces the legendary hero of medieval chivalry into the tale, while his daughter Freya invokes the Norse divinity of Northern love. The first manifestation of love is, in fact, a product of war and wrath, representing a form of contraction. The heraldic bird announces the arrival of the king and a foreigner, marking the beginning of eternity, the awakening of the queen, facilitated by the warmth of fire and love that unites the earth and sea. Thus, the night will end, and the realm of Fable will commence. This summary of the story highlights the main transmutations: the eternal present and the conjunction of opposites. Until this point, a long night prevailed, corresponding to the alchemical phase of *nigredo*, where everything is poised for future events, with the essential elements being fire and love. The volatile, the queen, remains imprisoned and asleep, while the earth and sea remain separated. The prophet of this rebirth is a bird, likely a symbol of the soul, as noted by Centeno: "a bearer of wisdom, is generally a vehicle" (1987: 54).[71]

---

[71] "portador de sabedoria, é em geral um veículo".

In a house, the children Eros and Fable are asleep. Eros is cradled by Ginnistan, who is also nursing Fable. Eros embodies Greek love from the South and connects to Orphic cosmogony, reinforcing the link between *Ofterdingen* and Orphism. In Orphic belief, everything begins with the primordial night and Protogonos-Phanes-Eros, the creator god, who is the first to emerge, not created but self-originated. As Miguel Herrero explains, "that the power of creation (conceived of as sexual in nature) is rooted in him alone" (2010: 299), since he emerged from the cosmic egg: the one who gives rise to all; recalling the Philosopher's Egg, in which the ouroboros is deposited and from which the blue flower springs. Eros sleeps in his cradle with a multi-coloured handkerchief, representing the *cauda pavonis*, the polychromatic phase of the alchemical work, which also refers to Heinrich's first dream, in which life was vividly coloured. The handkerchief covers the cradle so that Eros is not disturbed by the light of a scribe's candle residing there.

Ginnistan again reflects Meyer's second emblem: the earth, the nurse who nourishes the *filius philosophorum*, the child of the sun and moon. However, Ginnistan represents not only the earth but also water. As she is the daughter of King Luna, she must embody the element of water. Additionally, her name has an Arabic ring, emphasizing her exoticism, i.e., her position outside the centre of European mythology. As Debra Prager asserts, Ginnistan "alludes to the legendary Jinn (or genies) [...]. The Jinn holds an intermediary status between humanity and the divine [...] to inform and inspire poets, prophets, and soothsayers" (2014: 164-5). Thus, her origin recalls the eccentricity of Zulima and the Edenic paradise of poetry that reveals the mysteries of nature.

Ginnistan embodies the nourishing, maternal element more profoundly than Fable and Eros's own mother, who is perpetually occupied, lacking a name, and summoned away from nursing Fable almost immediately. In contrast, Fable shows more affection toward Ginnistan, and Eros too will demonstrate greater enthusiasm for his nurse; this is not surprising: fantasy, represented by Ginnistan, nourishes creativity, embodied by Fable, and love, represented by Eros. Additionally, the father maintains extramarital relations with Ginnistan.

Beside Eros stands a woman with the stature of a goddess, Sophia, who dips leaves into a black bowl of clear water, provided by the scribe.

Only a few words survive the water. Sophia sprinkles the same water over Ginnistan, Eros, and Fable, creating a blue mist from which strange images emerge. Conversely, if the water falls on the scribe, numbers and geometric figures appear. The ideal, as Klingsohr teaches, is the union of intellect and spirit. The water in the bowl destroys what is impure, which is why the scribe's writing—pure rationalism with numbers and geometries—does not survive. Gray notes, "a vessel filled with water—no doubt a representation of the alchemical retort" (2010: 28), suggesting that this bowl of water can reduce what is not noble to ashes. In contrast, when Fable writes, her paper survives Sophia's water. Uerlings highlights that "the figure of Fable [...] anticipates this messianic role of poetry" (1991: 417).[72] Fable can be considered the pure child, as Vaughan evokes, and represents the Philosopher's Stone guarded by the green dragon, mercury, Sophia. We previously identified this pure and philosophical child in Heinrich and the newborn child in the marketplace tale. Here, Fable is both Stone and Poetry because she already represents the transmutation of the universe into a magical poem and a fable of the senses, akin to Zulima's understanding of Arabic script.

In his notes, Novalis states that Sophia is "the holy, unknown. The realm of light and shadow live intermixed" (1945: 330).[73] She is the divine wisdom capable of reconciling opposites; indeed, her bowl is black and the water clear, and within the same room, Northern and Southern love coexist, just as Ginnistan, representing fantasy, is close to the scribe, the intellect. The Romantic project aims to reconcile binomials, merging Fichte's idealism with Böhme's theosophy. As Gray points out, the pietist Arnold Gottfried also writes that Adam, the hermaphrodite, since the separation of the sexes,

had been dissatisfied with his lot and had sought to be reunited with his other self, who was Christ, or the heavenly Virgin Sophia.[74] This

[72] "die Figur der Fabel [...] antizipiert diese messianische Rolle der Poesie".
[73] "das Heilige, Unbekannte. Das Licht und Schattenreich leben durcheinander".
[74] Sophia and the Virgin Mary are considered one and the same image in Paracelsian theosophy. Cf. Szulakowska (2017: 131-148).

was however yet another name for the Stone [...]. In so far, then, as the Stone represented the One and All. (2010: 222)

The identification of Christ with the Stone has been commonly asserted, based on Christian alchemy, as Gray observes from the writings of Basil Valentine, Robert Fludd and Heinrich Khunrath, a disciple of Böhme (2010: 20). Similarly, Sophia is identified with the Stone, and thus with Christ as well. Uerlings also corroborates this conception of Sophia, aligning it with Böhme's Sophia: "both are mediators to a maternal primordial ground of all things and appear as the heavenly bride and as wisdom" (1991: 499).[75]

The father of Eros and Fable appears with an iron rod found in the courtyard, capable of indicating the North. Ginnistan had shaped it into the form of a serpent biting its own tail, thus symbolizing the ouroboros and even anticipating the fate of the story.[76] As soon as Eros takes hold of the rod, he grows, reaching adolescence, and sets off with Ginnistan, who, on Sophia's advice, assumes the appearance of Eros's mother so that he does not feel attracted to her. The father of Eros, representing primordial attraction, who maintains a relationship with the fantasy figure Ginnistan, a mark of Eastern motherland, offers his son this phallic gesture which makes him grow. He thus passes on the legacy. In this sense, Ginnistan, as fantasy, directs the ouroboric process of transformation, a regenerative process that, in Böhme's thought, although he does not work with the ouroboros symbol, represents the seventh property, where "all the Properties are in temperature, as in one only Substance: and as they all proceeded from the unity, so they all return again into one ground" (1911: 30).

Markéta Balcarová states that the ouroboros in *Ofterdingen* represents the distillation cycle of the alchemical process (2016: 54), although the method of this distillation is not developed. Partially

---

[75] "beide sind Mittlerinnen zu einem als mütterlich qualifizierten Urgrund aller Dinge und erscheinen als himmlische Braut und als Weisheit".

[76] Liedtke (2003: 266) suggests that Novalis might have been familiar with the ouroboros, as he was a student of Johann Christian Wiegleb, who was the first to write an extensive history of alchemy and chemistry and had a particular interest in the ouroboros symbol.

disagreeing, we would rather consider renewal and expansion, as distillation pertains only to the *solve*, while the ouroboros also represents *coagula*. It destroys and constructs, as the *Märchen* will demonstrate. In any case, Balcarová might have intended by distillation, pertinently, a fusion of realities. In the process of volatilization and sacralization, the ouroboros also represents the mercurial substance, the most capricious and fluid of metals (Rampling 2014: 42), which can "kill" precious metals (43), fragmenting and dissolving them, to then perfect them, and, when reunited, obtain a perfect form. Marianne Beese, on the other hand, finds in the same symbol the synthesis of the return to the primordial origin (2000: 230): to distil in order to coagulate, to destroy profane time to return to a sacred time, from the real to the myth, which, in turn, becomes real. This encompasses the entire meaning of Klingsohr's *Märchen*, wherein the world is poeticized as romantics idealize.

It is also relevant to note that Ginnistan's transformation is due to Sophia's advice because she is responsible for the transmutation of matter; hence, the cup or retort is in her possession. As Centeno notes: "the quintessence of the universe is the Stone, it is the creative force in the form of the Eternal Feminine, the eternal creative principle, transmuter of life" (1983: 257).[77] We have also observed that the quintessence is blue, which links the flower, the Stone and Sophia at the heart of creation and transmutation. Ginnistan, fantasy and Eros take a vial of water from the cup and journey towards the realm of King Moon.

In the realm of Ginnistan's father, he presents his daughter with the key to a treasure: a lavish garden with never-before-seen animals and several castles in the air. A spectacle unfolds, featuring various images of different situations: natural phenomena, episodes of human life such as a couple in love, a battle, or a theatre performance. Suddenly, a blue river appears, merging sky and earth, and from this fusion emerges a flower, a lily, with a rainbow arching over the water and, at the top, Sophia with her chalice. Beside her stands a man with an oak crown and a palm of peace in hand. A petal of the lily falls, and seated on it is

---

[77] "a quinta-essência do universo é a Pedra, é a força criadora sob a forma do Eterno Feminino, do eterno princípio criador, transmutador da vida".

Fable, singing to the sound of a harp. In the cup of the flower is also Eros, leaning over a sleeping young woman; perhaps it is Psyche, Eros's great love. After the spectacle, Ginnistan takes Eros to bathe, and they engage in sexual relations.

King Moon, a mercurial realm, owns the garden of transmutation, an Edenic garden of revelations. His daughter Fantasia, the caretaker and mother, opens the garden: it is imagination, the mother and nurturer of all things, that grants access to transmutation. The spectacle presents various events that have appeared throughout the novel through dreams and tales, and whose symbols we have been developing. This spectacle, in this garden, is the synthesis of synthesis, a world within a world, creation within creation. Here, the entire alchemical process is revealed, as well as the creation of life and the world, identifying one with the other. Gathered in the lily flower, born from a blue river, are Sophia, Fable, and Eros: The Stone, the matrix, bringing together love and poetry, which sings and becomes music. Eros is, after all, a winged child, the same one from Heinrich's father's dream. He must fulfil the transformation of the universe and, to do so, he must merge with fantasy. Love bathes in the element of fantasy, the water, the caretaker, and the mother.

The symbolism of the lily is associated with the mystagogic impulse, when the conscious begins its journey into the inner world of the unconscious, guided by the *anima* or *animus*. Marie-Louise von Franz supports this reading when she notes of the lily, a recurring symbol in medieval alchemical texts, that it represents: "the flower of the field and the lily of the valleys; I am the mother of beautiful love, knowledge, and holy hope […] I am completely beautiful and without blemish […] I am the mediator between the elements, reconciling one with the other" (Jung 1979: 186).[78] Sophia is also described as a mediator, underlining the identification of her with the Immaculate Virgin, and later, with Mathilde. As I will discuss, this is a foreshadowing of Mathilde's role in Heinrich. In *Faust I*, Faust speaks of the alchemical operations his father

[78] "die Blume des Feldes und die Lilie in den Tälern; ich bin die Mutter der schönen Liebe, der Erkenntnis und heiligen Hoffnung […] Ganz schön bin ich und ohne Makel [...] Ich bin die Mittlerin zwischen den Elementen, die eines mit dem andern versöhnt".

performed, one of which was "united in the lukewarm bath of the lily" (v. 1043).[79] Regarding this passage, editor Erich Trunz comments that the lily is a symbol of mercury, the mercurial water that must bathe the sulphur to fix it (2010: 529).

Meanwhile, the *Märchen* continues with other actions. The scribe, representing intellect, seizes the house in the absence of the figures of imagination, imprisoning the parents of Eros and even incinerating the mother. This occurs as the sun itself collapses, establishing a correlation between the mother's death by flames and the destruction of the star. Up to this point the mother has not played a significant role but in this moment she becomes prominent: the sun, as a source of light and life, must die, just like the mother, light and life, for the process to continue. We may also consider that fire is both a creator and destroyer, much like God, light, and life. In any case, the loss of this feminine element causes, as we will now see, an imbalance in the world.

Upon encountering such a scene, Sophia flees with the alchemical vessel, and Fable descends a staircase behind Sophia's altar, discovering a world where light and darkness are reversed. The sun casts a shadowy light, and Fable finds herself before a cave guarded by a sphinx. The dialogue between them is significant, especially the sequence following the sphinx's question: "Where do you come from? - From ancient times. You are still a child. - And will forever be a child" (1945: 280),[80] until Fable asks: "Where is love? - In imagination" (280),[81] and the sphinx disappears. The eternal child, the Philosopher's Stone, poetry, from the golden age, responds about the whereabouts of love, her brother Eros, confirming that he is with Ginnistan in the world of the moon, in fantasy. The flight of wisdom with the alchemical vessel prevents the alchemical process from continuing. Poetry escapes to an inverted world, likely the world of the unconscious, a subworld where it must seek the answers it needs. Meanwhile, Eros, having become involved with the nurse-mother, becomes unrestrained, gaining wings and returning to a childlike state:

---

[79] "im lauen Bad der Lilie vermählt".

[80] "Wo kommst du her? - Aus alten Zeiten. Du bist noch ein Kind. - Und werde ewig ein Kind sein".

[81] "Wo ist die Liebe? - In der Einbildung".

the transformative and often chaotic force of love that leads to renewal and a return to original purity and innocence.

In the cave, Fable encounters the three Fates, her sisters, who maintain a black flame of oil burning steadily. She is given the task of spinning. While she spins, she sings for the dawn and for the unification of all threads into one, as a single heart and soul. The union she refers to is the same as that portrayed in the garden of delights of King Moon. The three Fates, or *Moirai* in Greek mythology, are the goddesses of destiny who control the thread of life for everyone. Clotho spins the thread of life, Lachesis measures its length, and Atropos cuts it, determining death. By meeting the Fates, Fable comes into contact with the forces of destiny and time, indicating a profound connection between poetry and the mysteries of existence and fate. The black flame is a vital, primordial force, distinct from the golden light, which belongs to a world already created and illuminated. The black flame represents the ancient and obscure chthonic forces. The act of spinning is one of waiting, resistance, and the creation of more time and history, reminiscent of Penelope's enduring patience while Odysseus is absent. Poetry spins, trying to ensure that its words, turned into music, govern fate from that point onward.

When the scribe appears, the black flame is extinguished, and the cave is illuminated by the normal world light, the light of reality. The intellect illuminating the darkness symbolizes Enlightenment itself. The life of the black flame represents the life of dreams, mystery, and the irrational, which tends to be domesticated and extinguished. The proposed tension between the vital, nature, and the reason of the self must be reconciled. For now, the unconscious, kept alive by the guardians of destiny, is being illuminated by rational content not filtered through Sophia's chalice. Without poetry, imagination, wisdom, and love, and with the light of the shadow of the unconscious, the tale undergoes a painful *nigredo*.

Fable manages to escape, finding a ladder to climb and a trapdoor that leads to the chambers of King Arthur. She asks him for a lyre, which he grants her. Upon finding Eros, she restores his natural childlike state with the sound of the lyre. Fable continues her journey and, looking up at the sky, sees Sophia with her blue veil. Novalis uses the same motif of the blue veil in a letter to his mother, relating it to the act of creation. Similarly, Hillman emphasizes that the Madonna's blue robe signifies purity born of wisdom. The lyre, invented by Hermes, given to Apollo, and passed on to Orpheus, has the transformative power to bring life and order to chaos. The legendary king possesses a lyre rather than a sword because the Romantic project is to poetize the world, not to fight and conquer. This universal poem must be created with Eros, the winged child, who allows the attraction of all impulses; Fable, who makes words sound like music; and Sophia, who holds the deepest knowledge of the world.

When Fable confronts the Sphinx again, it asks her among other things: "Who knows the world? - He who knows himself. - What is the eternal secret? - Love. - Where does it rest? - In Sophia" (290).[82] The first response refers to Novalis's poem "Kennst dich selbst" and the Oracle of Delphi. Knowing the world is only possible through the process of self-knowledge and the expansion of consciousness, as taught by Hermetic art. If Fable is an eternal child, love is, in turn, the eternal secret that rests in Sophia. Wisdom and love produce the very knowledge of the world, that is, of oneself. Knowledge of the world is obtained through eternal childhood, that is, through Fable. The Sophia-like knowledge calls for love and imagination (poetry, music, fantasy, fable) to come together to create a new world.

Perseus has the role of cutting off Eros's wings, that is, fixing the volatile, and as narrated, only in this way can the great work (i.e., alchemical work) be completed (292). Persia (the lineage of Perseus) influences Eros, the love of the South, Greece, and the entire West. Perseus, the hero combined with love, represents the tension between wrath and love, contraction and expansion that create the world. This is the same teaching offered by Klingsohr, in which the poet and hero are fused as a divine messenger. The persona controls the erotic, unconscious impulse to make it beneficial to the community. In a false etymology, we can relate Perseus and persona, as he cuts off the head of Medusa, who turns those who look at her into stone. This

---

[82] "Wer kennt die Welt? - Wer sich selbst kennt. - Was ist das ewige Geheimnis? - Die Liebe. - Bei wem ruht es? - Bei Sophien".

metaphorically represents integrating unconscious contents and channelling erotic impulses.

Subsequently, Fable returns to the palace and informs the king that there is no more linen to spin, as the inanimate [*das Leblose*] has once again become soulless, and it is now time for the animate [*das Lebendige*] to reign, using the material of the inanimate: "the inner is revealed and the outer is concealed" (293).[83] As we know, the black flame has been extinguished, and the scribe is producing without a soul, without the elements of imagination and wisdom by his side. Therefore, Fable claims the realm, utilizing the soulless material of the scribe. This opposition recalls the transition from *prima materia* to *ultima materia*, as Paracelsus describes: "the thing that becomes ashes / that is a substance: and although it is *ultima materia* and not *prima*, [...] it has stood in the living body" (2008: 308).[84] The material of the inanimate, the *prima materia*, which resembles Böhme's chaotic pre-created mass, serves as the foundation for the *ultima materia*, the created and living substance. As previously noted, the circular equation remains the same: the Stone is found if the *prima materia* is discovered, but it is only revealed in the making of the Stone.

The ouroboros is symbolically invoked, representing death that generates life, the destruction that creates. The real world is inanimate and lacks the thread for further weaving, and must be replaced by the *Märchen*, which is created and alive, full of infinite imagination. The image of linen being spun symbolizes the return of what was, yet never the same, as revealed by the ouroboric figure. However, there is no more linen to repeat the pattern of the inanimate. A new linen must be created to spin a new order, that of the animate. The revealed inner, the dream, is thus shown as the *prima materia* discovered, which, upon being discovered, becomes the Stone, exterior to the world. This Stone, once exposed, is again hidden, which leads to the conclusion, along with Mähl, that "if the world had previously become a dream,

[83] "das Innere wird offenbart und das Äußere verborgen".
[84] "das Ding das zu Eschen wird / das ist ein Substanz: und wiewol es ist Vltima materia und nicht prima, [...] sie ist / gestanden im lebendigen Corpus".

then now the dream should become the world" (1994: 412).[85]

Before Fable begins to weave for the rest of eternity, the new golden age, she returns home, where Sophia remains standing, with Eros in armour lying at her feet and his father in a coffin sleeping. Ginnistan proclaims Fable as the soul of life and tasks her with awakening the groom, Eros's father. She then calls forth Gold, which fills the coffin with lava, while Zinc constructs a metal chain around Ginnistan's chest. Characters like Gold and Zinc indicate that the realm itself is composed of the basic elements of the universe, thus susceptible to complete transmutation. Ginnistan leans over the groom, with her hand on his heart, and sees her image multiplied. As the chain touches the lava, the groom, whose body appears as a subtle liquid, awakens, and the metal solidifies, forming a clear mirror. Sophia deposits the ashes into her cup and ensures that the mirror will eternally preserve the archetypes, revealing the true form of things. Life and death unite in the cup, initiating the process of revelation. Everyone drinks from the cup and feels the presence of Eros's mother, who was previously incinerated by the scribe.

Eros, the love, prostrated before wisdom, and the father of love lying dead: the latency of vital forces, the decay of matter. Imagination, fantasy, once uncontrolled by Eros, commands the poetry, Fable, to revive the vital forces. She is the heroine who rebalances the world, which had been in imbalance since the death of her mother, and who brings back light and life, that is, the sun. For this reanimation, the perfection of Gold must bathe the father, as Heinrich dreamed, while Zinc purifies this transformation, guiding the forces of imagination, Ginnistan, to the dormant love. He is now the groom in the alchemical equation to be sublimated by his bride. In this subtle transformation of matter, the bride, Mercury multiplies, expands, and conceives, while the groom becomes solidified metal. What was liquid, dormant, and latent now awakens and hardens: the erection, the desire for conjunction. The father, seen as the sense, the direction, because he provides the rod that indicates the North, is liquefied and solidified with gold, giving rise to the rebirth of a new sense of the world.

[85] "[es] war die Welt vorher zum Traum geworden, so sollte nun der Traum Welt werden".

Thus, the mirror is formed, the creation of the philosopher's stone, or *lapis philosophorum*, which reflects the true nature of things and preserves the eternal archetypes. According to Jungian thought, the ego is a mirror for the unconscious (Samuels 1989: 76), since the ego is a part of what is known of the personality and helps define what remains unknown. The ashes of the entire *nigredo* and subsequent *albedo* are placed into Sophia's cup, so that the integration of all transformed and purified elements can occur. Uerlings confirms the rebirth through the drinking of Sophia's ashes, which, for him, represents a spiritual baptism, in line with Böhme's theosophical thought (1991: 499). The archetypes, the primordial images, are preserved in this mirror, and only by drinking from the cup, which is identifiable with the unconscious, is access permitted.

Sophia concludes that the world was created through the pains of all and that in the tears of the cup of life, the ashes dissolve. By drinking from it, the heavenly mother dwells in everyone, so that each child may be born for eternity. Collective suffering gives rise to a saline solution, which, as we have seen, represents the sacrifice of Christ in Pietistic tradition. In this case, this redemptive tear purifies the calcined ashes to regenerate the matter. The conjunction of the fiery element, the ashes, and the watery element, the tear, of the king and queen, as shown in various alchemical treatises, leads to the birth of the Elixir or Philosopher's Stone.

By drinking the regenerated matter, the nurturing aspect of the heavenly mother will infuse spirit and life into creation, integrating the divine dimension into all beings, enabling them to attain eternity, the ultimate goal of the alchemical work. This conception appears in Ulmannus's alchemical treatise, *Buch der Heiligen Dreifaltigkeit*, where the Virgin Mary and Christ are considered one, symbolized by the blue lily. When the substance is fixed through condensation, it represents the Mother; when it volatilizes through dissolution, it represents the Son (1986: 36-7; 210). The Christian sacrifice present in the tears dissolves into the cup of the heavenly Mother, who resides in all who drink from it. The motif of the sacred feminine, extensively developed in various mystical and religious traditions, is here recreated as a communion with both Christian and Orphic elements (Kuzniar 1992: 1200-1202). Instead of communing with the body of Christ, it is the body of the mother that is emphasized, revisiting the theme of the hermaphroditic, allowing even the masculine to give birth. Moreover, Novalis's interest in the hermaphroditic figure is evident in his fragments; for example, "the man is in a certain way also woman, just as the woman is man" (1946: 259),[86] suggesting that both male and female exist within each being, and rejecting a falsely romantic notion of seeking the other half as a sign of incompleteness. The quest for the other does not serve to fill a void but to multiply the work.

When Sophia affirms that the man gives birth to the mother, she evokes the time of the Virgin Mary becoming a mother by bearing Christ within her, as well as the earth becoming maternal matter through the alchemist. The transmuter makes matter his mother. In Böhme's view, it is the alchemical marriage that creates the androgyne. The reconciliation of the masculine with the feminine is also the union of the human with the divine, of finite consciousness with the immaterial Sophia, wisdom. The alchemical work produced within us is, therefore, the revelation of this masculine or feminine, not always obvious, within us. In this revelation, an internal marriage occurs that allows the creation of the androgyne, the philosopher's stone, the true perfection. We are imperfect matter, as long as we have not achieved the state of being both masculine and feminine simultaneously. This will be an interesting topic for further discussion, considering gender issues in alchemy, Romanticism, and contemporary contexts.

Finally, Fable and Eros depart to rescue Arthur's daughter, Freya, whom Eros loves. They witness various loving couples uniting, flowers and trees growing, and all animals, plants, and stones singing and speaking. The ancient Hero gives his sword to Eros so that he may awaken Freya. Upon reaching her chambers, Freya transfers a spark to Eros's sword, and "the plume of his helmet rose" (1945: 298),[87] until he drops the sword and kisses Freya, sealing their eternal union. The galvanic theory, which describes the production of electricity in heterogeneous bodies without friction, metaphorizes the erection, and we witness another successful conjunction.

[86] "der Mann ist gewisser-maaßen auch Weib so wie das Weib Mann".
[87] "Helmbusch wallte empor".

Additionally, it is significant that Freya is seated on a throne of sulphuric crystal. Sulphur, for Böhme, represents the struggle of an unstable element to transcend itself through revelation, in order to become fixed. Böhme writes, "wherein the fiery life burns, the oil lies; and the quintessence lies in the oil, viz., the fiery Mercury, which is the true life of nature, and which is an effluence from the word of the divine power and motion, wherein the ground of heaven is understood" (Böhme 1911: 19). Thus, the sulphuric crystal throne on which Freya sits symbolizes purity and final transformation, in which the unstable element (sulphur) becomes fixed and achieves its quintessence. This union represents the culmination of an alchemical process whereby the fiery life (Eros) finds its purest and most divine expression (Freya), resulting in eternal harmony and union, symbolizing the perfection and balance of elements.

King Arthur and the heart priestess (1945: 301), Sophia, marry Eros and Freya, bestowing upon them the royal diadem and the lily, thus celebrating Spring. The diadem represents eternity and perfection, while the lily symbolizes Sophia herself. There is no need to reiterate the reinforced symbolism of the diadem and lily, which is also connected to the arrival of Spring. The totality of divine wisdom, the Philosopher's Stone, has been given to them. Interestingly, Spring is slow to arrive for Heinrich, as his grandfather humorously noted, corresponding to Freya from the North. In contrast, Mathilde, from the South, is represented by Eros.

Thus, Fable can weave the eternity of love into an unbreakable thread of gold, as prophesied by the heraldic bird at the beginning of the tale. Fable sits on the wings of the Phoenix and rises to the heavens, while spinning her golden thread and singing of the eternity of love, veiled by Sophia. The winged, pure child ascends, creating the universal musical language of love. The Phoenix is the result of the solution of ashes and tears, as it is the mythical creature that is reborn from its own ashes: death that leads to life. All prophecies have been fulfilled through the power of love, as the creative and unifying element of being.

Each dream, story, and experience has been complexified until reaching the extent and intention in Klingsohr's *Märchen*, which Novalis himself declares, in the *Fragmente des Jahres 1798*, as having "in the novel [a] geometric progression" (1946: 24).[88] The *Märchen* ends, as does the first part of *Heinrich von Ofterdingen* and as does the world as it is known. Littlejohns observes that in the second part, "empirical reality is totally supplanted and Heinrich moves only in a supernatural world where the restrictions of time and space have disappeared" (2004: 69). Liedtke refers to this suppression of temporal and spatial constraints as a leap into a mythological time, facilitated by the alchemical process (1996: 135). Mähl confirms that *Ofterdingen* tends toward the form of myth, rejecting the rules of probability, causality, and linearity (1994: 441).

Klingsohr has constructed a transcendental world, and Heinrich learns from him "den Zauberstab der Analogie" (1946c: 25), "the magic wand of analogy", a term used by Novalis in *Die Christenheit oder Europa*. In this way, Klingsohr has initiated Heinrich into his vocation as a poet, and for poetry to be the transmuter of his world, Mathilde will introduce him to the conjunction of opposites. The creation of a world through imagination, love, and poetry has been learned and awakened. A verse from the poem "Astralis", in the second part, indicates that Fable begins to spin (Novalis 1945: 304), transposing Klingsohr's tale into reality, where the new world falls, the ordinary becomes marvellous, and light turns into darkness (303), as had happened in the cave with Fable, signalling that the dream reigns.

2.5. THE WORK SUPPLANTS REALITY

> There is no past to yearn for; there is only an eternally new one, which shapes itself from the expanded elements of the past.[89]
>
> Goethe zum Kanzler Friedrich Müller (1823)

---

[88] "im Roman [eine] geometrische Progression".

[89] "Es gibt kein Vergangenes, das man zurücksehnen dürfte, es gibt nur ein ewig Neues, das sich aus den erweiterten Elementen des Vergangenen gestaltet."

When Heinrich contemplates Mathilde on the first night at his grandfather's house, during the ongoing celebration, he thinks, "her face was like a lily inclined towards the rising sun" (237).[90] Two elements are invoked: the lily and the coming dawn. Just as the blue flower had metamorphosed into Mathilde's face, so now she becomes the flower, surely blue. If Mathilde's face was not yet known, the flower was also unknown. At this moment, Heinrich understands that the face is Mathilde's and that the flower is a lily. I would add that the lily, which emerges from both heaven and earth, represents Mathilde, the flower of poetry. Both are fruits of Klingsohr. Love and poetry are united in Mathilde to unite with Heinrich.

After the young woman reveals that she can play the guitar, Heinrich's fascination with her intensifies. This leads to their first kiss, and soon Heinrich feels the same sensation he experienced when he saw the blue flower in his dream. He concludes that the face he saw in the centre of the flower, in the chalice [*Kelch*], botanically speaking, was Mathilde's, just as she appeared in the hermit's book. This chalice also appeared in the *Märchen*, referring to the place where the flower was located, where Fable was seated. Fable was linked to Mathilde-the-lily, both being daughters of the same father, the creator Klingsohr. As Heinrich acknowledges, Mathilde represents his "innermost soul, the guardian of my sacred fire" (245),[91] bringing him the dawn and the rising sun, for "the night is over" (246),[92] thus ending his *nigredo*, his long night of learning and deconstructing the self, in preparation for renewal. The innermost soul confirms the role of anima, as has been noted. As the guardian of his sacred fire, she plays the same role as the sphinx. The questions posed by the sphinx could similarly be asked by Mathilde to Heinrich: where he is from, where is love, who knows the world, what is the eternal secret. Heinrich needed Klingsohr to answer these questions, derived from the character Fable in the story, as she, as Heinrich will assert, is his key.

Heinrich was truly Klingsohr's disciple, and for this reason,

---

[90] "eine nach der aufgehenden Sonne geneigte Lilie war ihr Gesicht".
[91] "innerst Seele, die Hüterin meines heiligen Feuers".
[92] "die Nacht ist vorüber".

Mathilde wishes: "what a blessed creature I would be if you were as faithful as my father" (261),[93] also revealing that her mother died shortly after she was born. Klingsohr was Mathilde's world; she becomes his creation and now, as a creature, yearns to transfer that same power to Heinrich. Regarding this projection, it is interesting to refer to Martha Helfer's study on Romanticism and Gender Studies, in which she reflects: "while it is true that Romanticism casts the definition of the male artist in terms of woman, the true source of Poesie, it is equally true that this female figure is subordinate to and dependent on an exoteric male figure" (2004: 243). Mathilde is not a poet; she is poetry itself. She is both a creature of the poets Klingsohr and Heinrich and the creator of their art. Without her, there would be no poetry. However, she still feels dependent on her creators, as without poets there would be no manifested expression of poetry. Heinrich understands this, realizing that Mathilde is "the visible spirit of the song, a worthy daughter of her father" (1945: 245).[94] This interdependence also exists in alchemical conception: why has there always been disagreement about whether everything originated from water or fire? Because it came from both. Without their conjunction, life could not be conceived, nor could metal be transmuted, nor could the Stone be made.

In this new phase for Heinrich, a new dream emerges. It is dawn when the young man falls asleep, during the bluish night before the sunrise. In his dream, he sees a green meadow, a blue river with a boat on it, and Mathilde in the boat, wearing a crown, rowing and singing. Suddenly, the boat begins to spin, and Heinrich throws himself into the river to help Mathilde, but he is swept away by the current. Mathilde sinks along with the boat. The young man's heart stops, and when he regains consciousness, he finds himself on solid ground, although unfamiliar, with a spring, flowers, and trees. He hears Mathilde calling him and realizes that the tranquil waters of the river flow above them. When he asks where they are, she replies: "at our parents' home", "bei unsern Eltern" (247).

---

[93] "welches selige Geschöpf wäre ich, wenn du so treu wärst wie mein Vater".
[94] "der sichtbare Geist des Gesanges, eine würdige Tochter ihres Vaters".

In the dream, they have reached their homeland, meaning that both have died and inhabit the age of gold, as inscribed on the stone tablet regarding the Hohenzollern couple. The river and Mathilde refer to the water element, which is transformative, uniting two banks, two opposites—life and death, present and future in this case. Centeno adds that

> the river is still the formless chaos, the aggressive, violent masculine principle; its waters are those of an overflowing unconscious, threatening because it is not ordered, because it is not integrated. Only with the definitive joining of its two banks will the river become more perfect. (1976: 22)[95]

This interpretation fits well with the dream, as it represents the unification of the present with the future, life with death, creating the mythological time Heinrich seeks through poetry. His unconscious is overflowing because it is still in the process of organizing recent content. Mathilde, crowned, signifies the perfect time to be fulfilled— the sleeping queen in the father's *Märchen*, who becomes Sophia at the end.

After the first lesson with Klingsohr about the relationship between nature and soul, and body and light, Heinrich referred to Mathilde as sapphire, gently illuminating everything, being clear and transparent like the sky (1945: 249). As mentioned, the blue flower is known in Hermetic philosophy as the sapphire of the hermaphrodite. Thus, Hohenzollern advised never to take one's eyes off the stars. By looking at them in the sky, one would always be looking at Mathilde, and in turn, looking at oneself. As hermaphrodites, they are one and the same.

Klingsohr invites Heinrich to learn the guitar with Mathilde, and the young man asks her if she would accept him as her eternal disciple (253). More than just a guitar teacher, Mathilde is the master of Heinrich's soul. This confirms her role as the mystical guide of the

---

[95] "o rio é ainda o caos informe, é o princípio masculino agressivo, violento, as suas águas são as de um inconsciente transbordante, ameaçador porque não ordenada, porque não integrado. Só com a ligação definitiva das suas duas margens será o rio tornado mais perfeito".

poet. As a gesture of acceptance, the girl offers Heinrich the rose she wears on her chest. The rose holds the same significance as the chalice. The earth is a golden chalice in Heinrich's father's dream, love is a chalice that, when drunk, opens the gates of heaven, as sung in the grotto Heinrich visits with the miner, and finally, the chalice of Sophia, the alchemical womb that purifies all suffering and gives birth to the philosopher's stone. Thus, the rose is a transmuting and mercurial symbol. The historian of science Hans-Werner Schütt notes that from an alchemical and Rosicrucian perspective, the rose and dew establish an affinity that is reflected in the etymology of some languages to this day, with "dew", "ros", being the masculine counterpart to "rosa" in Latin (2000: 506). For instance, in French, "dew" is "rosée", and "rose" is "rose". In Spanish, "dew" is "rocío", and rose is "rosa", phonetically similar.

Mathilde accepts being the mercurial bath, the dew of Heinrich's sublimation. Later, she says: "Ah! Heinrich, you know the fate of the roses!" (1945: 261).[96] Indeed, he knows it, for he has already dreamt of this destiny. Roob, in his study of *Uraltes chymisches Werk* by Abraham Eleazer, the legendary teacher of Nicholas Flamel, relates the rose to the "water, white as the moon, called python (a code name for *Mercurius vivus*)" (2006: 327). This also highlights the ouroboric quality of this relationship. Mathilde, being both a rose and a lily, refers to Maria Hohenzollern. For now, the mercurial, transmuting aspect of the rose in relation to the dew interests us. This is because dew is also a mercurial water, moistening what is dry and giving life to what is dead. Therefore, dew, as a rose, is feminine, the chalice that is also a flower and receives the dew, the fertilizing tear. From this union, perfection is born, named love and wisdom, or better yet, Sophia. It is also worth noting that love, as union, is represented by Eros, and by rearranging the letters, we get the word "rose".

In German, "dew" is "*Tau*", a word frequently used by the Rosicrucians (Roob 2006: 513), who regarded it as the nectar, the mercury of the philosophers (267). Salt fixes the dew, the body fixes the volatile, and together they form an alchemical pair. This is because

---

[96] "Ach! Heinrich, du weißt das Schicksal der Rosen!"

dew contains a "crystalline salt endowed with the power of harmony" (304). Interestingly, the word "*Tau*" in German resembles the Chinese *Tao*, and as Centeno cites from the *Tao Te Ching*, "one Yin, one Yang, and we have the Tao" (Centeno 1983: 243),[97] which is nothing more than stability and harmony. Vaughan writes that the mercurial water, the dew, is "permanent Water, the spirit of the body, [...], the mineral water, the dew of heavenly grace, the Virgin's milk, the bodily Mercury" (1919: 205). Furthermore, Kirchweger states about the dew: "dew, rain, snow, hail, frost, but fundamentally it is the real seed, the true reborn Chaos [...], out of which all sublunary subjects are born, preserved, destroyed and reborn" (1921: 100). In summary, just as dew is a solvent of matter that brings about rebirth, the rose is the "dispensadora de vida", "dispenser of life" (Centeno 1991: 72). Both are what Novalis and F. Schlegel term the *menstruum universale*, the universal solvent of the alchemists, which merges the real and the imaginary (Dye 2004: 238).

After finishing the lesson with his master, Heinrich is alone with Mathilde, and it is important to highlight her feeling that the pair have known each other since unthinkably distant times [*undenklich*]. This evokes the theory of Platonic reminiscences or the primordial origin of the hermaphroditic being, which is the cornerstone of all Ofterdingen. This Platonic root is further observed when Heinrich tells her that her "earthly form is but a shadow of this image" (262),[98] assuring her that this form cannot be fixed in nature, as it is still immature, and because she is an eternal archetype [*ewiges Urbild*], reminiscent of Goethe's Eternal Feminine. It is believed that Goethe told Beethoven that "the eternal feminine, that is the music which mysteriously harbours life and spirit in its womb" (Marx 1902: 212),[99] which aptly suits Mathilde, not only because of her connection to music but also because the spiritual life is in her womb, highlighting her maternal quality, which is further deepened.

[97] "um Yin, um Yang, e temos o Tao".
[98] "deine irdische Gestalt ist nur ein Schatten dieses Bildes".
[99] "das ewige Weibliche, das ist die Musik, die das Leben, den Geist, geheimnisvoll in ihrem Mutterschoße birgt".

Mathilde continues to express her feelings, making her speech a profession of faith: she states that she is willing to die for Heinrich. The philosophical mercury that Mathilde represents makes her the dragon that must drink its own poison, to die and give way to the Stone. She is the green dragon guarding the treasure that the pure child must discover, as mentioned earlier. It is from her, dew and rose, that the saltpetre is extracted to ignite the philosophical fire—Heinrich called her the guardian of the sacred fire. As I noted earlier, it is Böhme who identifies sound with mercury and saltpetre. Heinrich sighs: "she will dissolve me in music" (1945: 245).[100] The mercurial water, the dewy rose with its saltpetre-music, dissolves the *prima materia* and transmutes it. Mathilde also represents the ouroboros, the *Mercurius vivus* called python: self-destruction, fertilization, and renewal in the circular movement of the serpent. As already known, only death leads to life, in the light of alchemy. Or, as Gray notes: "the only road to perfection was through death, either physical or spiritual" (2010: 227).

Heinrich considers that only now does he understand what it means to be immortal, and both make their vows: "Ah! Mathilde, even death will not separate us. — No, Heinrich, where I am, you will be. — Yes, where you are, Mathilde, I will be eternally [...]. Mathilde, we are eternal because we love each other" (1945: 261).[101] The one resides within the all, embodying love that guides toward eternity. It is eternal, infinite, and circular in nature. To him, Mathilde is "the heaven that supports and sustains me" (260-1),[102] and therefore he does not take his eyes off her, as Hohenzollern prophesied. She is close to becoming the celestial Sophia, to whom Heinrich prays: she is the saint who intercedes for him with God, revealing Him (261). As he himself inquires, "What is religion but an infinite accord, an eternal union of loving hearts?" (261).[103] It is this eternal union between consenting

---

[100] "sie wird mich in Musik auflösen".
[101] "ach! Mathilde, auch der Tod wird uns nicht trennen. — Nein, Heinrich, wo ich bin, wirst du sein. — Ja, wo du bist, Mathilde, werde ich ewig sein [...]. Mathilde, wir sind ewig, weil wir uns lieben".
[102] "der Himmel, der mich trägt und erhält".
[103] "was ist die Religion als ein unendliches Einverstandnis, eine ewige Vereinigung liebender Herzen?"

hearts that will allow Heinrich to penetrate "into the sanctuaries of life, into the Holy of Holies of the mind" (262).[104] There is no separating the poetic, alchemical, spiritual from the sexual element.

Heinrich's final desire is for this love to transform into wings of fire that will carry him and Mathilde to the celestial homeland (262), thus transforming them into the Phoenix. These wings also evoke those that Eros gains when he engages sexually with Ginnistan, for it is worth remembering that Klingsohr is "der Vater der Liebe" (260), "the father of love", i.e. Eros, Freya, Heinrich, and Mathilde. Mathilde, in turn, feels a secret flame that transfigures and dissolves the earthly chains [*irdische Banden auflösen*] (263). The alchemical operation is no longer confined to the perfection of metal and the human, microcosmically, but also to the perfection of their connection with their celestial form, in the macrocosm. On the one hand, the fire present in Heinrich dissolves and volatilizes Mathilde's water. On the other hand, the earthly chains dissolve to give way to spiritual chains. This dissolution is their *nigredo*, as intuited by Heinrich, the calcination of metallic alloys, i.e., of the earthly chains.

Both feel their conjunction: "my whole being shall merge with yours" (263).[105] She dissolves him into music, he dissolves her earthly chains. The poem "Astralis" expresses the longing for a more intimate and total fusion through love (302) in a unity superior to the one: an annihilating and autopoietic force, the zero degree of creation, represented in the ouroboros. The ouroboros can be seen in this union in various forms: fecundity, eternity, conjunction of opposites, and repetition, for as Heinrich states, "love is an endless repetition" (263).[106]

The young couple seal their vows with hugs and kisses, thereby constituting the alchemical pair. The eternal repetition is also the eternal present, and as Goethe writes in the poem "Vermächtnis": "then the past is constant, / the future vividly anticipated, / the

---

[104] "in die Heiligtümer des Lebens, in das Allerheiligste des Gemüts".
[105] "ganzes Wesen soll ich mit dem deinigen vermischen".
[106] "die Liebe ist eine endlose Wiederholung".

moment is eternity" (1963: 513).[107] What accentuates the conjunction is the fact that Heinrich is more than just a disciple of Klingsohr. He is like a son, which deepens Mathilde's projection, as previously observed. Heinrich addresses the master as "lieber Vater" (257), "dear father", and "[...] seinen neuen Vater" (264), "his new father". In this sense, Heinrich symbolically functions as Mathilde's brother. This detail is alchemically significant because, as Gray observes, "to achieve perfection, the brother and sister must be joined together, and thus the sister becomes a wife. [...]. To 'marry the sister' was to overcome duality, and to achieve oneness with the parent of all things" (Gray 2010: 223). The androgynous, the hermetic hermaphrodite, thus has the conditions to form.

The second part of the work, titled "The Fulfilment [die Erfüllung], the Cloister [das Kloster] or the Forecourt [der Vorhof]", opens with the poem "Astralis," with which the empire of love [der Liebe Reich] is inaugurated through conjunction: "not separately anymore only Heinrich and Mathilde, / United both into one image" (303).[108] This is the image of the hermaphrodite, the primordial being, the *prima* and *ultima materia*, the Philosopher's Stone, representing the very image of God, the divine spark present in all beings, from humans to stones, as the same poem further indicates: "one in all and all in one, / God's image on herbs and stones / God's spirit in humans and animals" (304).[109] The universal family, dreamed and prophesied, is realized.

The poetic subject appears to be the child of this conjunction when they state, "there I felt the pulse of my own life / for the first time" (302).[110] Being the child of this conjunction means being the hermaphrodite itself, or Heinrich and Mathilde as one. Thus, the poetic self also says: "and as love / lost itself in deeper delights, / I awakened more and more, and the desire / for a more intimate,

---

[107] "dann ist Vergangenheit beständig, / das Künftige voraus lebendig, / der Augenblick ist Ewigkeit".
[108] "nicht einzeln mehr nur Heinrich und Mathilde, / Vereinten beide sich zu einem Bilde".
[109] "eins in allem und alles in einen, / Gottes Bild auf Kräutern und Steinen / Gottes Geist in Menschen und Tieren".
[110] "da fühlt ich meines eignen Lebens Puls / zum ersten Mal".

complete merging / became more urgent with each moment" (302).[111] Hence the desire of the united to merge more and more, as if there were a unity superior to the one. And, indeed, there is: the zero, the null but active potency, the degree zero of creation, the primordial Eros of the Orphics that promotes the unity between the uncreated and the created.

In this path, this one being is "der Mittelpunkt, der heilige Quell" (302), "the centre, the holy source". This original centre relates to the concept of *axis mundi*, the *axis* that transcends time and space, creating the eternal present in the ouroboric movement, as the poem corroborates: "no more order according to space and time, here future in the past" (304).[112] It is where the source from which flows the water of Sophia is found. Alchemy teaches exactly how to achieve this movement of the eternal wisdom of the present, as reinforced by the alchemist Fabre, "who teaches [us] to know the centre of all things; which in Divine language is called the Spirit of Life" (2009: 9-10),[113] the pulse of life itself, as the poem reveals.

The line "die Fabel fängt zu spinnen an" (1945: 304), "the fable begins to spin", marks the transition from Klingsohr's tale to reality. More precisely, it signifies a radically ontological shift in the world, for "a new world breaks in / and darkens the brightest sunshine, / [...], / and what was formerly commonplace / now seems strange and wonderful" (303).[114] The creative power of poetry, of Fable itself, is further affirmed: "the world becomes a dream, the dream becomes the world" (304).[115] The transformation accomplished transcends human

---

[111] "und wie die Liebe sich / in tiefere Entzückungen verlor, / erwacht ich immer mehr, und das Verlangen / nach innigerer, gänzlicher Vermischung / ward dringender mit jedem Augenblick".

[112] "keine Ordnung mehr nach Raum und Zeit, hier Zukunft in der Vergangenheit".

[113] "qui enseigne de connaître le centre de toutes choses; qu'en langage Divin l'on appelle l'Esprit de vie".

[114] "es bricht die neue Welt herein / und verdunkelt den hellsten Sonnenschein, / [...], / und was vordem alltäglich war, / scheint jetzo fremd und wunderbar".

[115] "die Welt wird Traum, der Traum wird Welt".

spirit by far. It was the spirit of the world that underwent transformation, stemming from the conjunction of poetry and the poet of love: the tale surpassed reality. This overcoming is due to poetry aligning itself with the alchemical operation, as Mähl notes: "poetry becomes the medium of natural interconnectedness and takes on the historical legacy of repressed traditions of hermetic philosophy, especially alchemy" (476).[116] What was once merely alchemical—the transmutation of nature—now becomes explicitly alchemically poetic.

The poem asserts: "the primal play of nature begins, / it reflects on every powerful word, / and thus the great world soul / moves everywhere and blooms infinitely" (304).[117] This passage emphasizes the role of the poet as a direct descendant of the primordial Adam, the name-giver and creator, the first transmuter who coagulates the volatile by giving it a name. Thus, as the poem suggests, every being reflects in the whole. Microcosm and macrocosm correspond. Heinrich acquires the words he lacked through his dissolution with Mathilde. As Burkhard Dohm states, "For Novalis, the universe is entirely an analogue of human beings in body, soul and spirit" (2000: 373),[118] which Novalis himself affirms in *Glauben und Lieben*, and which we have had the opportunity to quote: "my beloved is the abbreviation of the universe, the universe is the elongation of my beloved" (1945b: 50).[119]

The poem concludes, and immediately the image of a pilgrim climbing a mountain is presented. The time he finds himself in is now mythological and primordial, marked by his embrace of the rock and the fact that the rock begins to speak, followed by a tree. The tree prophesies that if he plays the lute, a girl will appear. The pilgrim

---

[116] "die Poesie wird zum Medium des Natur zusammenhangs und tritt darin die historische Nachfolge der verdrängten Traditionen hermetischer Philosophie, insbesondere der Alchemie an".

[117] "das Urspiel jeder Natur beginnt, / auf kräftige Worte jedes sinnt, / und so das große Weltgemüt / überall sich regt und unendlich blüht".

[118] " das Universum völlig ein Analogon des menschlichen Wesens in Leib, Seele und Geist".

[119] "meine Geliebte ist die Abbreviatur des Universums, das Universum die Elongatur meiner Geliebten".

recognizes, in the tree's voice, the voice of Mathilde, and from this indication it becomes apparent that he is Heinrich. A ray of light appears, and he sees in the distance the figure of Mathilde. After this vision, he reflects on "the bitter pain of an unspeakable loss" (308),[120] which allows us to understand that Mathilde had died, as he had dreamed.

After singing, honouring his love for Mathilde, the pilgrim opens his eyes and there is a girl, Cyane. Part of the dialogue established between them is worth quoting because it invokes the alchemical content that has been explored here. The pilgrim asks the young woman:

"Who told you about me?" asked the pilgrim. - "Our mother." - "Who is your mother?" - "The Mother of God." - "Since when have you been here?" - "Since I came out of the grave." - "Have you died before?" - "How could I live?" - "How do you know me?" - "Oh! From old times; my former mother always told me about you." - "Do you have another mother?" - "Yes, but it's actually the same one." - "What was her name?" - "Maria." "Who was your father?" - "The Count of Hohenzollern." - "I know him too." - "You must know him well, for he is also your father." - "I have my father in Eisenach." - "You have more parents." - "Where are we going?" - "Always home." (311-12)[121]

Death as a generator of life has already been addressed. Without it, the operation does not progress. The Mother of God symbolizes the

---

[120] "die herbe Pein eines unsäglichen Verlustes".

[121] "Wer hat dir von mir gesagt? Frug der Pilgrim. - Unsre Mutter. - Wer ist deine Mutter? - Die Mutter Gottes. Seit wann bist du hier? - Seitdem ich aus dem Grabe gekommen bin. - Warst du schon einmal gestorben? - Wie könnt ich denn leben? [...] - Woher kennst du mich? - O! Von alten Zeiten; auch erzählte mir meine ehmalige Mutter zeither immer von dir. - Hast du noch eine Mutter? - Ja, aber es ist eigentlich dieselbe. - Wie hieß sie? – Maria. - Wer war dein Vater? - Der Graf von Hohenzollern. - Den kenn ich auch. - Wohl mußt du ihn kennen, denn er ist auch dein Vater. - Ich habe ja meinen Vater in Eisenach. - Du hast mehr Eltern. - Wo gehn wir denn hin? - Immer nach Hause."

celestial Sophia, the earthly Mary, or the paradisiacal Eve, as Böhme called her (2013: 92). What must be highlighted here is this multiplication of being in unity. Having multiple fathers and mothers resonates with Orphic reincarnation, but the essential idea is that of circularity and self-fecundity, the ouroboric principle, which promotes the idea that everything refers to a common origin, a single foundational matter that has merely divided into opposites: feminine and masculine, light and darkness, water and fire, sky and earth, sun and moon, etc. The path, the alchemical work, is always towards home, a return to the unity of matter and spirit, because, as Eirenaeus Philalethes (George Starkey) affirms, "the main ground for the possibility of transmutation is the possibility of reduction of all Metals, and such Minerals as are of metallic principles, into their first Mercurial matter" (Starkey quoted in Gray 2010: 16). The mercurial matter is Sophia, on a celestial level, as Mathilde is on a terrestrial level, and both fulfil the function of expanding consciousness in the discovery of the *prima materia*, which enables the creation of the Philosopher's Stone.

The two young people go through the forest until they find the old man's house where the young woman is staying. The young woman addresses the pilgrim as Heinrich, already knowing his name, and introduces the old man, Sylvester. He is the old miner known to Heinrich and is also the old man who sheltered Heinrich's father, as was initially told, confirming this fusion of identities, the multiplicity within unity. At this point, it is important to reflect on the characters as archetypal variations. Sylvester (the miner-hermit) is indeed a variation of Hohenzollern and Klingsohr, in different spheres, representing the same ideal image: the first contemplates time in nature, the second in his book, within himself, and the third contemplates it through the union of the two expressions, interior and exterior, in his words. As Gerhart Hoffmeister summarizes, the characters are "variations of the Absolute [...]. Thus, when readers look at any one figure, they already are within the inner circle of the final message" (2004: 87). He gives the example of Zulima-Mathilde-Cyane, which, in fact, Novalis must have thought of when writing in the notes to the work about the concept of "Dreieiniges Mädchen" (1945: 331), the trinitarian girl. Indeed, the first sees him as similar to her brother, poet and musician, the second crowns him as a poet, while the third is the fruit of his music and poetry.

From the conversations with Sylvester, we highlight Heinrich's question: "[…] must the mother die so that the children can thrive, and is the father to remain alone at her grave in eternal tears?" (314).[122] This question echoes the final part of "Astralis": "the body is dissolved in tears, / the world becomes a wide grave, / into which, consumed by anxious longing, / the heart falls as ashes" (304-5).[123] Besides recalling motifs evoked in Klingsohr's tale, Heinrich seems to insinuate that he and Mathilde had at least one child. However, as I have also noted, the child of the conjunction is also the very hermaphroditic being, and in this sense would still be Heinrich. In any case, the theme of the deceased or absent mother is recurring: in the tale of Atlantis; Hohenzollern's wife; no mention of Heinrich's grandmother; the omitted mother of Heinrich since the party at the grandfather's house; Mathilde's mother; the sleeping queen and the incinerated mother of Eros in the *Märchen*; and Mathilde herself. This thought leads to Heinrich's conclusion that soul/psyche/heart [*Gemüt*] and destiny [*Schicksal*] are two names for a single idea, which makes me recall the fate of the roses that Mathilde declared to her beloved. The fate of the roses is their soul, mercurial water, dew, volatile that dissolves, sublimates, conjugates, dies, and creates. Dies and becomes, as Goethe would say. The fate of the roses represents "a life of completeness, where the human and the divine no longer oppose each other and harmoniously integrate" (Centeno 1991: 72).[124] Klingsohr merges the real and the imaginary, Mathilde merges the human and the divine.

At another moment in the conversation, Heinrich considers the possibility that the earth harbours a primal childhood, and the clouds represent a second childhood, a return to paradise, and that dew will be a product of this, melting over the first childhood. In a way, this

---

[122] " […] mußte die Mutter sterben, dass die Kinder gedeihen konnen, und bleibt der Vater zu ewigen Tränen allein an ihrem Grabe sitzen?"
[123] "der Leib wird aufgelöst in Tränen, / zum weiten Grabe wird die Welt, / in das, verzehrt von bangem Sehnen, / das Herz als Asche niederfällt".
[124] "uma vida de completude, em que o humano e o divino deixaram de se opor e se integram harmoniosamente".

resembles Mathilde's return with a second form., her ascent and connection to the symbol of dew. The second childhood, a new form of creation, produces the matter with which the alchemical work begins and that will be used to transmute the first childhood, the still chaotic and undifferentiated matter. The use of the verb "to melt" is particularly apt, not only because of the image it conveys of dew forming in the clouds and appearing on the earth but also because of the shared action in the alchemical process.

The path of alchemy, as I have already emphasized, is the path of expanding consciousness, and Sylvester even proposes this when he reflects, "only the person of the cosmos is able to perceive the relation of our world" (321).[125] The quest for absolute consciousness, which is related to Fichte's studies, is of the same order as that expansion, in which the universal self-awakens, the microcosm transmutes into the macrocosm, and vice versa, forming unity. Regarding this, Mähl observes that "the ultimate goal of unity, the abolition of the non-I through the I and the restoration of the absolute, non-I and I encompassing transcendental I (as the sphere of identity) represents an infinity goal" (1994: 289).[126] Thus, primordial nature conceives everything as a transcendental self-consciousness, containing the self and the other, the self and the non-self, and also the self of the non-self: mind and nature united, soul and destiny, responsible for the creation of the world.

The wisdom of Sophia accesses that consciousness, the centre, the *axis mundi*. In this regard, Heinrich admits to Sylvester that the Fable is the key to his current world, and consciousness: "this meaning and world-generating power, this seed of all personality, appears to me like the spirit of the world poem" (321).[127] And, as Centeno points out, the

---

[125] "nur die Person des Weltalls vermag das Verhältnis unserer Welt einzusehn".

[126] " […] daß das letzte Einheitsziel, die Aufhebung des Nicht-Ichs durch das Ich und die Wiederherstellung des absoluten, Nicht-Ich und Ich umgreifenden transzendentalen Ichs (als Sphäre der Identität) ein Unendlichkeitsziel darstellt".

[127] "dieser Sinn und Welten erzeugende Macht, dieser Keim aller Persönlichkeit, erscheint mir wie der Geist des Weltgedichts".

symbol of the key is necessary "to be able to open [...] and enter the philosopher's rose garden. The key is also called the 'Stone'" (1991: 65).[128] The Fable is the Stone, the key that opens the destiny of the roses and creates the eternal present. Sylvester corroborates this statement, adding that consciousness "is the essence of humans in full transfiguration, the heavenly primordial human" (1945: 322).[129] Thus, for Heinrich, the poet lives at the threshold of this primordial world, and consciousness appears in him in the form of his poetic discourse. Furthermore, in this sense, the young man reflects that the revelation present in religions is also present in the fables written by poets, with myth and history being intimately related. Mythological time, the eternal present, becomes the time of history in the poetized world, where the word is revelation, transmutes, and inscribes its being into the world. The first alchemy, already expressed, that of life, begins with the very creation *fiat Lux* or the Novalisian *Licht macht Feuer*, as previously mentioned.

Evola determines that the hermetic consciousness, renewed by the liberation of the anima (here, the death of Mathilde), expands the present moment and the life of the adept (2006: 183). This movement of expansion is described by the symbol of the ouroboros, "principio della 'chiusura'" (49), the "principle of 'closure'", by which the transcendent and the immanent unite, given that transcendence

is conceived as a way of being compressed into it as one thing, which has a dual sign: [...] it is identity and simultaneously poison, that is, the power of alteration and dissolution; it is both a dominant principle (male) and a dominated principle (female) [...] – and thus "androgynous". (49)[130]

---

[128] "para poder abrir [...] e entrar no roseiral dos filósofos. À chave também se chama 'Pedra'".

[129] " [...] ist der Menschen eigenstes Wesen in voller Verklärung, der himmlische Urmensch".

[130] "d'essere compresso nela 'cosa una', la quale 'ha dúplice segno': [...] è identità e simultaneamente veleno, cioè potenza di alterazione e di dissolvimento; è ad un tempo principio dominante (maschio) e principio dominato (femina) [...] – e quinde 'androgine'."

It is this conjunction of an androgynous time, we would say, that is realized with Mathilde. Also consider the poisonous identity proposed by Evola, as the mercurial dragon must taste its own poison and die from it, in sacrifice and creation, as Mathilde embodies.

The postscript by Tieck reveals the guiding idea of the book, that the age of miracles has ended because the world itself has become a true miracle, animated by the spirit of poetry and moved by the sidereal man, the result of the kiss between Heinrich and Mathilde (1945: 341). Tieck recounts Novalis's ideas for continuing Heinrich's journey, one of which was for him to remain in a cloister where monks form a Masonic lodge, guarding the sacred fire of young souls and teaching Heinrich everything about death, the philosopher's stone, and magic. Thus, the path of the poet-alchemist would continue.

Beyond all the initiatory teachings, the fragments presented by Tieck and the entire story of the first part highlight the hymn to love that figures prominently in this work. On this point, it is important to emphasize the idea of the alchemical process, including transmutation, self-knowledge, the conjunction of opposites, the elevation of being, the discovery of divine wisdom and the universal self, which aligns with the action of the verb to love, which makes everything into a single being: "to cling firmly to the beloved, / to receive him inwardly, / to be one with him" (346).[131] As one of the poems, which was to be included in the second part, asserts: "pleasurably the streams part, / for the struggle of the elements / is the highest life of love / and the heart's own heart" (345).[132] This alchemical conception is diametrically opposed to Burckhardt's view, which argues that "with its impersonal observation of the world of the soul, alchemy is closer to the path of knowledge, or gnosis, than to that of love" (Burckhardt 1991: 33).[133] Novalis proves the contrary, by uniting destiny and soul, and, along with Böhme and the entire Gnostic tradition, merging knowledge and

---

[131] "am Geliebten festzuhangen, / ihn im Inneren zu empfangen, / eins mit ihm zu sein".

[132] "lustern scheiden sich die Fluten, / denn der Kampf der Elemente / ist der Liebe hochstes Leben / und des Herzens eignes Herz".

[133] "com a sua observação impessoal do mundo da alma, a alquimia aproxima-se mais da via do conhecimento, ou gnose, do que da do amor".

love. In Novalis, the alchemy of the word is the alchemy of love, because "the figure of divine Sophia, which is none other than the Word, the Logos, the structure of all existence, represents in Böhme the universal archetype of the masculine and feminine, in conjunction" (Centeno 1987: 73).[134] In *Ofterdingen*, there is a poetic transmutation of the world through love.

In this world, Heinrich will experience further allegorical adventures, such as the quest for a hidden eagle, which leads him to find a golden key, stolen by a raven, which then guides him to the heart of a mountain and an encounter with the first stranger who spoke to him of the blue flower. The references to the world of alchemy maintain the purpose of uniting opposites to return to a primordial nature. The tension between the raven, representing *nigredo*, and the eagle, representing *albedo*, is drawn from the alchemical wedding of Rosenkreutz, though here it is a dove rather than an eagle, despite their similar symbolism in this context (Andreae 1973: 55).

If the first part of *Ofterdingen* represents the acquisition of experiences through the journey of the inner house, the second part is dedicated to the departure from this house to the outside world. However, in this return to the world, Heinrich makes it his own inner house: in Tieck's words, "an old homeland in his soul" (1945: 349),[135] leading him to a desire for transfiguration, opening the doors to the realm of Fable. Hence, the second part is titled "Fulfilment" and the first "Waiting" or "Expectation", as it is in this phase that he achieves his arrival in the world of Sophia, guided by Mathilde.

Heinrich finally finds the blue flower: it is Mathilde, who had died, holding a carbuncle while standing beside a coffin. The carbuncle is red, as is the final phase of the work. Mathilde is the Stone and, thus, holds the carbuncle. Her position beside the coffin implies that from death comes life, as previously noted. There is also a girl present, the daughter of the two young people, representing "the primordial world,

---

[134] "a figura da Sophia divina, que não é senão o Verbo, o Logos, a estrutura de toda a existência, representa em Böhme o arquétipo universal do masculino e do feminino, em conjunção".

[135] "eine alte Heimat in sein Gemüt".

the golden age at the end. Here, the Christian religion is reconciled with the pagan" (1945: 351).[136] Thus, she is the same pure child, evoked at the beginning, who discovers this treasure that is the primordial world of the golden age.

In the second part, Heinrich also dreams of the overlaying of the narratives from the first part onto his life. To be more precise, according to Klingsohr's tale, Heinrich's father would be the sense [*Sinn*] and his mother the imagination [*Phantasie*], the grandfather the King Moon. Klingsohr would be the king of Atlantis, from the merchant's tale, and Heinrich would be the poet from the first merchant's tale. As Novalis points out, the merchants' stories about the figure of the poet may become Heinrich's destiny (331). Each end finds its counterpart and closes in on itself, ouroborically speaking, consuming itself, with the purpose of creating the absolute reality. Heinrich fulfils his poetic vocation by consuming poetry and projecting it into the external reality, until everything becomes *Märchen* and poetry: *multiplicatio* and *projectio*.

The ouroboros is the symbol of symbols, as I have tried to indicate throughout this study. I would even venture to say that the ouroboros is the symbol of the symbol itself. The Greek verb "*symballein*", "to unite", "to gather", also has the noun "*symbolon*", "a token of recognition". As Centeno notes, "it is the symbol that allows establishing such connections between thought and dream, between consciousness and the unconscious [...]. In the symbol, there is no opposition" (1987: 52).[137] It is also about engendering the union of the inner path with the outer, the self with the non-self, the self with the world. In the ouroboros, there is no opposition; the contraries have already dissipated, recovering a time prior to the fall of the primordial Adam, a time, as I proposed earlier, androgynous.

Heinrich teaches how this annulment of oppositions is done, with the aim of following the winding path of the Stone, sculpted in the

---

[136] "die Urwelt, die goldne Zeit am Ende. Hier ist die christliche Religion mit der heidnischen ausgesöhnt".

[137] "é o símbolo que permite estabelecer tais ligações, entre o pensamento e o sonho, entre a consciência e o inconsciente [...]. No símbolo não há oposição".

balance between knowledge and love, by merging knowledge and love. It is not just the love of knowledge, nor the knowledge of love, since that would strengthen one while weakening the other, but it is knowledge in love and love in knowledge. Only in this way can the total image of Sophia be conceived, in the penetration of the two. Mathilde was love and poetry, being the daughter of the father of love and eternal poet, and Heinrich similarly became so, being initiated by him, being adopted by him, and ultimately being fused with her. Indeed, the image of the androgyne emerges: "symbol of the unification of opposites [...] results from the sublimation of the *prima materia*, the unconscious, by the alchemical fire, the transforming consciousness" (Centeno 1987: 57).[138] Klingsohr, the alchemical fire, worked on Heinrich until his transforming consciousness, Mathilde, came to him to make the world an hermetic androgyne.

However, one should not confuse the androgynous with the ouroboros, but rather incorporate the former into the latter. That is to say, the androgynous signifies the union of the masculine and feminine opposites in the alchemical operation. In contrast, the ouroboros represents the reconciliation of opposites as powers, intentional forces of creation. Ultimately, the ouroboros encompasses the entire meaning of alchemy, which has been consistently emphasized: transmutation, from self-destruction to self-fecundity, the eternal return to primordial nature, the *conjunctio oppositorum*, the correspondence between microcosm and macrocosm, and it also symbolizes the various stages of the alchemical process, from the fixed to the volatile and the fixation of the volatile. This is understandable, as the alchemical process is structured as a process of creating life, that is, its construction illuminates the entire symbolism of the ouroboros. Böhme's image of the wheel as God continues to evoke the ouroboric circle. As Zarathustra, through Nietzsche's pen, exclaims: "Everything anew, everything eternal, everything interconnected, intertwined, beloved, oh so you loved the world!" (1907: 402).[139] This phrase is the

---

[138] "símbolo da unificação de opostos [...] resulta da sublimação da prima matéria, o inconsciente, pelo fogo alquímico, a consciência transformadora".
[139] "Alles von neuem, Alles ewig, Alles verkettet, verfädelt, verliebt, oh so liebtet ihr die Welt!"

corollary of the ouroboric notion, including the very image of the draconian serpent eternally chained and coiled.

Heinrich teaches us to develop the human potential, through imagination, to become the creator of a world, that is, to become the fecundating Stone. Thus, the ouroboros presents itself in Heinrich as the alpha and omega, the beginning and end, which annul the time and space of consciousness, exalting the eternal present, because it has reached the centre, the *axis mundi*, the space of the time of creation.

THE WORK CONTINUES

> I have always dreamed and attempted
> something else, with the patience of
> an alchemist, ready to sacrifice all
> vanity and satisfaction, just as one
> used to burn one's furniture and the
> beams of one's roof to feed the
> furnace of the Great Work.[1]
> Stéphane Mallarmé to Paul Verlaine (1885)

Romanticism allows for the expansion of a pansophical attitude, in what Benjamin called the romantic continuum of the arts: "the unity of forms leading to the total, unique, and self-reflective work of art" (Schefer 2005: 20).[2] The fusion of poetry with prose, the universalization of this movement to poeticize everything, *sinphilosophy, simpoetry,* and the treatment of the subject as the centre of perception and formulation of reality are well-emphasized in *Ofterdingen.* Idealism, magical in the case of Novalis, seeks to reconcile the human self and the self of nature, identical and tensioned, one as the postulate of the reality of the other, the non-self. Through imagination, which creates and poetizes, and through reason, the domesticated understanding, the idea of the absolute is achieved: reconciled tensions, the human and the divine fused.

---

[1] "J'ai toujours rêvé et tenté autre chose, avec une patience d'alchimiste, prêt à y sacrifier toute vanité et toute satisfaction, comme on brûlait jadis son mobilier et les poutres de son toit, pour alimenter le fourneau du Grand Œuvre."

[2] "l'unité des formes conduisant à l'oeuvre d'art totale, unique et ipsoréflexive".

The Romantic project and Novalis's philosophical movement intersect with the fervent pietism of the time. Thus, the movement of poetizing the world and reuniting being with its nature also becomes a gesture of returning to a primordial unity existing in the golden age, identified with the chiliastic promise of Christ's millennial reign. Indeed, the infancy of humanity acquires special relevance for Novalis, as it evokes an Adamic, Edenic, Christian, and even Eastern, specifically Indian, condition. Sanskrit and Indian literature, so popular at the time, provide a cradle for a primordial, musical and creative language. These considerations are all formulated in *Ofterdingen*.

Novalis discovers alchemy through his own relationship with chemistry and mineralogy, through Böhme's pietistic mysticism, and through Neoplatonism in Hemsterhuis. His alchemical thought is intertwined with pietistic influences and a strong desire for reconnection with the universe through poetry and love. The desire for an eternal present, where past and future are conjugated into a *geistige Gegenwart*, the spiritual present, becomes pronounced in Novalis's alchemical quest. It is no longer merely a matter of transmuting his spirit or reality itself, but of creating conditions for the promised paradise to be realized in life and for humanity to fulfil its creative potential.

Novalis's idea about the inoperativeness of being in its objectification can be understood in alchemical terms as an invitation to continuous transformation and the pursuit of a new unity that transcends dualities. Alchemy, with its focus on transmutation and the union of opposites, offers a rich metaphor and a practice that resonates with Novalis's critique of Fichte, suggesting that the true essence of being is dynamic, mysterious, and always in the process of becoming. The Romantics, like Novalis, greatly valued alchemy for its overcoming of dualities, striving for the absolute through the attainment of a new unity. Alchemy seeks integration and synthesis that transcends mere objectification.

In alchemy, the process of transformation involves the deconstruction (*solve*) and reconstruction (*coagula*) of matter. This process can be seen as a way to go beyond stagnation, seeking a new

135

essence or a purer essence through alchemical work, seeking a new essence or a purer essence through alchemical work. Both Novalis and alchemy acknowledge the mystery and ineffability of being. Alchemical knowledge is not entirely rational or objective: it is often symbolic, intuitive, and esoteric. This insight aligns with the view that the essence of being cannot be fully captured by rational objectification.

Novalis suggests that the existence of being is a phenomenalization, an active creation of images by being itself. Similarly, in alchemical tradition, the use of symbols and images represents internal and universal processes. Images such as gold, the philosopher's stone, mercury and sulphur are used to express profound truths about the transformation and essence of matter and spirit. Alchemy is, in many respects, a science of creative imagination, whose symbols are not mere reflections but creations that preserve and transmit hidden knowledge. The idea that being becomes an image in thought and is preserved through these images can be compared to the alchemical process of transmutation. The concept of *solve et coagula* (dissolve and coagulate) in alchemy can be seen as a metaphor for the continuous creation and transformation of the images of being. The *prima materia*, or being, is dissolved, that is, phenomenalized, and then coagulated, meaning it is preserved in a new form.

In alchemy, raw matter is transformed into something purer and higher through a symbolic and material process of decomposition and recomposition. This purity has often been associated with Platonic values such as beauty, justice, and truth, and has been traditionally understood from a moral perspective. However, let us consider a more concrete example from alchemy, the case of metals. The purity of a metal refers to the proportion of the metal present in an uncombined state, free from other elements or compounds. In other words, it is the measure of the absence of impurities within the metal. The higher the purity grade, the closer the metal is to being composed entirely of atoms of that specific metal, with minimal presence of other elements or contaminants. It is this process of purification that alchemy seeks, and which led Jung to develop his process of individuation: a psychological developmental process whereby an individual becomes a complete and autonomous self, confronting their shadow—i.e., impurities, the conscious and unconscious aspects poorly integrated into the personality; becoming aware of projections and illusions to achieve greater clarity and harmony; finding their anima/animus, i.e., the feminine and masculine aspects of the psyche; and achieving the total realization of the self, the closest to our true self.

Novalis argues that the purity of being can never be accessed fully because its images are only presence, not essence. In alchemy, there is the relentless pursuit of the philosopher's stone, which represents ultimate perfection and purity but is often described as unattainable or elusive. The alchemical quest can be seen as an attempt to achieve this essential purity of being, even though the philosopher's stone may symbolize an unreachable ideal.

Thus, alchemy reflects the tension between the phenomenalization of being and the quest for its pure essence. Through the novel *Heinrich von Ofterdingen*, we observe this Jungian journey, through which the main character works towards his realization until achieving the level of purity that, in his case, is the vocation of a poet. However, the Jungian reading is not the only way to understand alchemical purity. The association of alchemy with the arts, philosophy, and literature suggests that purity is also found in the discovery of one's own language by each artist and thinker. All the work of observation, analysis, destruction, and renewal of thought in the creative process to achieve something original and autonomous pertains to the attainment of this alchemical purity—not associated with what is merely beautiful or good.

Novalis proposes that true social and political transformation comes from an inner revolution whereby the individual recognizes themselves through interaction with the Other. This echoes alchemical thought, where personal transformation, known as the Great Work, is essential for achieving a more perfect state of humanity. Alchemy emphasizes the importance of self-knowledge and integration of both the shadowy and luminous aspects of being to achieve complete transformation. This process of individual integration and transformation is seen as essential for collective transformation.

The fragmentary nature inherent in the second part of *Heinrich von Ofterdingen* aligns with the Romantic ideal of infinite repetition, where the fragment itself becomes absolute, allowing readers to chart their own textual path (Schefer 2001: 79). The novel is necessarily a fragment "because the Absolute can only be represented or constructed in an infinite finitude" (Hu 2007: 131).[3] Thus, the questions that arise allow us to explore possible conclusions, reflecting the correspondence between the microcosm and macrocosm. What is the relationship between the dream of the blue flower and the dream of the Philosopher's Stone? What type of quest is Heinrich undertaking? Why do Klingsohr and Mathilde appear at an advanced stage of Heinrich's learning? What was missing for Heinrich that his two alchemical guides provide? What is the power of the love between Heinrich and Mathilde? What is the significance of Mathilde's death for Heinrich?

Heinrich's quest for wisdom and love unfolds through the development of his vocation as a poet and the poetic vocation of the world. The blue flower, whether inspired by Indian traditions or Western alchemy, symbolizes the union of wisdom and love, which, in their Gnostic and Kabbalistic forms, converge in the divine Sophia with an alchemical twist. These elements are essential for the creation of the Philosopher's Stone. The search for these three images represents a pursuit of self-knowledge. This search begins unconsciously, through dreams, using symbols well-known in the hermetic tradition: essentially, the sea, death, rebirth, the forest, the cave, light, and the blue flower. Thus, the search is primarily an inner journey. It is through this inner voyage that the external, conscious journey is realized: without the dream, there would be no sharing of the father's dream, Heinrich would not remain hopeful and eager, and his mother would not have swiftly suggested the journey to Augsburg. This symbolic, suicidal movement allows for the rebirth of a new path of learning. Much like Zosimos, he continues the alchemical operation he dreams of while awake. Indeed, for Novalis, the artist is a somnambulist awake, in whom fantasy and reason interpenetrate (Oliveira 2014: 112). We recall Bernardo Soares: "I do not know if I

---

[3] "weil das Absolute nur in einer unendlichen Verendlichung dargestellt bzw. konstruiert werden kann".

am dreaming when I live, if I live when I dream, or if dreaming and life are mixed and intersected in me, forming my conscious being through interpenetration" (Pessoa 1982: 229).

Although Heinrich's journey is physically realized, taking him to his mother's homeland, it remains fundamentally an inner journey. The tales of other poets and the experiences drawn from the lives of others (Zulima and Hohenzollern) expand his consciousness. It represents another way of perceiving the undifferentiated, the formless individuality, becoming differentiated through the formative sociability of the self, in order to return to the undifferentiated unity, yet absolute and conscious. In this manner, Heinrich learns the truth of dreams, the golden value of the poet, and the prophetic and transformative capacities of his music and poetry, as well as the Eastern origins of poetry and the poet. In summary, he learns that the poet is an alchemist, in the transformative quality of poetry—"alchemy that dissolves the constraints that subject man and the world, while simultaneously achieving an infinite approximation between man and the absolute, a continually provisional reunion that aspires to completeness" (Oliveira 2014: 134).[4] However, Heinrich has not yet learned, nor could he at this stage without a master, how to craft his poetry and discover poetic inspiration. In this respect, Klingsohr and Mathilde are essential to the development of his potential.

Heinrich needed inner development before he could receive Klingsohr and Mathilde into his life. Only through an awareness of the value of his learning and his path could he fully appreciate the level of initiation he encounters initially with the eternal poet. Moreover, Klingsohr and Mathilde are found in Augsburg, but this destination only becomes feasible because Heinrich undertook his inner journey. Thus, they could only appear at an advanced stage of the young poet's inner discovery. Furthermore, the journey to Augsburg to meet his masters evokes a return to the maternal womb, given that it is the birthplace of his mother. The womb here is identifiable with Sophia,

---

[4] "alquimia que dissolve os entraves que sujeitam o homem e o mundo, ao mesmo tempo em que realiza uma aproximação infinita entre o homem e o absoluto, reunião sempre provisória que aspira à completude".

the creator-matrix of the world. As previously discussed, to achieve the Philosopher's Stone, one must return to the maternal womb, considered the primordial origin, where the *prima materia*, the ouroboric egg, resides, and there undergo a symbolic death, i.e., initiation. Klingsohr and Mathilde awaited Heinrich at the origin of his ontological initiation.

Broadly speaking, it can be concluded that Klingsohr bestows wisdom and Mathilde bestows love upon Heinrich. By associating fire with his first guide, Klingsohr becomes the key to the work and is perpetually present in the process of destruction and renewal. Klingsohr is the eternal poet, a symbol of the eternity of poetry and its self-fecundating power, being also the father of love, Mathilde, and Fable—the key to the hermetic work, which merges the real and the imaginary, the universal solvent. Klingsohr teaches Heinrich the transmuting power of imagination combined with word and understanding, as well as demonstrating the power of love through his *Märchen*. Thus, his guidance transmutes reality, fulfilling the millenarian promise, inaugurating the golden age, so that his disciple may become the promised Orphic and Adamic poet, one who will unite the universal family in the verb to love, restoring the alchemical poetics to its original musical, Eastern, contemplatively ecstatic form.

Mathilde, embodying both love and wisdom, merges with Heinrich, forming the hermaphroditic figure and opening an inner pathway for him to reach the *axis mundi*. The power of the love between Heinrich and Mathilde is of the same order as the ouroboros: it leads to the unity of the *prima materia*, constructing this hermaphroditic figure by uniting the masculine and feminine polarities, reformulating the eternal present. Heinrich's depth is revealed by Mathilde, who is music and poetry personified, the blue flower Heinrich dreamed of, the lily, symbol of mercury: she is his entelechy, his soul that enables him to realize his full potential. Her mystical love initiates Heinrich into the original language that contains the wisdom of self-knowledge. The chalice of Sophia, symbolized by the rose in the *Märchen*, collects the tears of sacrifice, i.e., the symbol of the cross. The Rosicrucian symbol is represented by dew, the universal solvent that sublimates the matter. Mathilde's death is symbolically the sublimation of this mercury, the poisoning of the dragon, so that the differentiated may return to the undifferentiated, yet with the eternal consciousness of having reached the *axis mundi*, of having united with Sophia.

The Orphic register found in Heinrich is characterized by his qualities as a poet: a mediator of all nature, where the inner realm of poetry and music recreates nature and enables descent into the underworld, i.e., the unconscious, to transmute the real. Alchemically, this descent is equated with returning to the maternal womb because returning from the world of the dead is a return to life, to the origin. Orpheus, aware of the differentiated, the existential abyss separating him from Eurydice, attempts to reunite with her, reintegrating into himself the unconscious content that is her memory. The myth speaks of Orpheus's failure to rescue his beloved because he looked back. Was this impatience that destroyed the alchemical process or a confrontation with the shadow that led him to live with the gift of prophecy? Returned to the world of the living, he suffers the dismemberment of the volatile: the Maenads tear him apart, leaving only his head. Orpheus's head, representing intellect and imagination, remains active, floating down the river (*prima materia* and purifying water) to Lesbos, continuously reciting his prophetic poems with his lyre. The lyre is symbolically associated with poets and musicians. The head is buried by Dionysus in his temple on Lesbos. It is the *prima materia* of alchemists that must be found and regenerated to create divine wisdom, Sophia, which is the Philosopher's Stone.

Orpheus is the bard representing the struggle for the restoration of primordial unity, the hermaphroditic figure. He exemplifies the ouroboric movement: destruction, renewal, circulation, and prescience. Rubification symbolizes total rebirth in a fertile, creative, complete, and perfect unity. It is perfect because it integrates the unconscious rather than repressing it, allowing for the reunion of opposites and returning to its Adamic lineage of naming creation. With Heinrich, this is clearly visible, as previously discussed: his dream of communicating with stones, plants, and animals is realized; a wholly new world is created, even though everything and everyone is a product of eternal return. Heinrich reconciles in time the Orphic head, obtained through Klingsohr's initiation, and the lyre, symbolically obtained with Mathilde. Her death, having fulfilled her mission, is evidenced by the entire world being transformed into *Märchen*, or a worthy dream of Heinrich. *Märchen* and dream are the raw materials that transmute the real. As Martin Mees reflects, "dream seems to give shape to the 'transmuted' real through romantic imagination, a space governed by paradoxical and combinatorial logic [...] essential to the alchemical birth of a form, the solve and coagula of poetic matter" (2019: 167).[5]

From Klingsohr's *Märchen* and the transformation of reality after its narration, we infer that the material world, in poetic creation, loses density and opacity, gaining transparency—an attribute given to Mathilde and clearly a mark of the revelation granted by Sophia. The spirit, in turn, gains such density that it becomes corporeal. This mirrors what happens in alchemy: the volatilization of the fixed and the fixation of the volatile. However, the issue is not the transcendence of matter, the discovery of a spiritual world beyond our own, but rather the perfectibility of matter through the instruments of knowledge and love. What is transcended, in terms of overcoming, is not an otherworldly realm but ourselves. Novalis teaches through Heinrich that we are the creators of our spiritual reality, based on the tension between meaning and feeling. Since we are all united with Sophia, we all have the potential of Fable, the creative potential. We do not ascend to God; rather, God descends into us. In other words, we marry Sophia in this very material world.

What Novalis practices in *Ofterdingen* and what was contemplated by alchemy aligns with what Gilles Deleuze later articulated: that the work is an idea that takes forms, nuances, and movements, reconfiguring what can be seen and said, i.e., reconfiguring the empirical. To think one's own thought, as Heinrich learned; the matter that thinks, works, and reconfigures its own matter, as alchemy aims to

---

[5] "le rêve semble donner figure au réel 'transmuté' par l'imagination romantique, espace régi par une logique paradoxale et combinatoire [...] indispensables à la naissance alchimique d'une forme, le solve et le coagula de la matière poétique".

teach. In this sense, the chemical-alchemical rupture has left alchemy orphaned of descent: let us not forget that it is the child who gives birth to the mother; it is the child who makes the mother a mother. In this orphancy, starting in the seventeenth century, the poetic transmission of natural knowledge, used by alchemy, is recovered for the fertile field of art, especially literature.

The transmutative capacity of alchemical matter is reflected in its linguistic work, as well as its significant capacity to absorb various ways of thinking about reality. Therefore, the hermetic attribute has shifted from great initiatory societies to Romantic, modern, and contemporary poetics, as Hugo Friedrich teaches us in his work *Die Struktur der Modernen Lyrik*. Adorno also discusses hermetic poems in *Ästhetische Theorie* that distance themselves from the material and empirical dimension of reality. A poetically alchemical language reveals and conceals simultaneously, disorientating its function of communication under the sign of the magic of language. All this was strongly propelled by Novalis, who established connections between alchemy, chemistry, mining and language, setting the stage for the French symbolists, as well as avant-garde movements such as Surrealism and Expressionism, and even a significant portion of nineteenth- and twentieth-century German poetry.

Heinrich von Ofterdingen revitalizes the legacy of Orpheus, recovering a language that enchants and transforms reality. Furthermore, Novalis reinforces the divine aspect of reality. Reality is real because it is divine, as Novalis asserts: "God wants gods" (1946: 88).[6] Everything converges, from the Orphics to the alchemists and from them to the Romantics, towards the unity of all with all. To know the *prima materia* of alchemy is a condition for this movement, for the union of matter with consciousness. For this purpose, language is the means of overcoming, uniting matter and consciousness in the word. For the Romantics, as for the alchemists, reality is language that, transformed into poetry, allows for absolute and spontaneous freedom, the appearance of the One, which Nietzsche will later present as Dionysus. As Heinrich learns and experiences, the poetic is an

[6] "Gott will Götter".

ontological category, an original experience lived by the being from within itself. As the mystical poet Ibn Arabi thinks, poetry is "the language of love, for being able to express the infinite" (Albarracín 2016: 235).[7]

The symbol is hermetic to the uninitiated and transparent to the initiated, which aligns with Eliade's conclusion that the symbol is polyvalent (1952: 17). Therefore, in the consciousness of the differentiated self, which begins to recognize the symbol, there is the possibility of returning to the undifferentiated, completing the ouroboros. This movement is also rooted in alchemical tradition: it is the transition from the hermetic to the hermeneutic. Thoth (Hermes) signifies "in the first case to mix, to soften through blending; in the second case to gather into one" (Durand 1969: 348):[8] disjunction, conjunction, unity. Heinrich becomes aware of the differentiated self in the Hohenzollern grotto, as he gazes at the illustrated book and sees himself in it. The recognition that he is present, as in the book, representing the past in a future moment, evokes the eternal present, the nullification of time and space in consciousness, as previously mentioned. When he meets Mathilde, the one he will unite with, he is ready to return to the undifferentiated, to a primordial origin, with himself, with her, and with nature.

This circular and temporal movement is also characteristic of the ouroboric and is present in alchemical tradition: Bonardel reminds us of Thoth,

> who, extending in his own way the mythical lineage of Adam, urged every man to rediscover within himself the perfect Nature of the primordial Man by beginning the cycle of spiritual regeneration initiated by Hermetic revelation. (2002: 24)[9]

[7] "el lenguaje del amor, por ser capaz de expresar lo ilimitado".

[8] "dans un premier cas mêler, adoucir par le mélange; dans le deuxième rassembler en un seul".

[9] "qui prolongeant à sa manière la filiation mythique d'Adam, engageait tout homme à retrouver en soi la Nature parfaite de l'Homme primordial en entamant le cycle de la régénération spirituelle initié par la révélation hermétique."

By attributing to Thoth/Hermes the paternity of language and alchemy, we create a fellowship between poets and alchemists. More than that, we aim to conclude that the application of alchemical operations may yield greater results when considered in the context of artistic and literary creation, in the language of the self.

For Centeno, "alchemy is the art that best helps to decode the hidden path of literary creation [...]. The matter of works, whether alchemical or literary, is the matter of life" (1987: 7).[10] In Klingsohr's *Märchen*, the ouroboros is represented by the magnetic iron the lover carries to seek the north, symbolizing the issue of poetic creation and its activity (Balcarová 2016: 37): the quest for the meaning of literary matter is pursued through imagination, Ginnistan, and creation as an act of love, hence the connection between it and Eros. One of Hermes' teachings in his *Corpus Hermeticum* is the revelation that the alchemical work and its meaning are within each person, which is why alchemy has been compared to artistic creation in its internal process, where the created work leads to the artist's own rebirth (Burckhardt 1991: 29). This is one way to conceive of the relationship between alchemy and art, given that "alchemical cosmology contains within it a theory of being, an ontology" (32),[11] which expresses the process of transmutation of each being.

However, considering the creation of the artistic work as necessarily linked to the transformation of the artist himself involves incorporating the non-artistic experience into this equation, substituting the creature for the creator. It is quite different to propose that the creator is also a creature, and that the creature, the work, is also a creator. Both emancipate themselves through the very alchemical process of the verb as Rimbaud envisioned: "they [the poets] were seeking was, literally, an *alchimie du verbe*, [...] transmutation of speech and transfiguration of language" (Agamben 2017: 126). Despite Agamben's previously mentioned pessimistic view regarding the success of the Romantics in achieving the alchemy of the verb

[10] "a alquimia é a arte que melhor ajuda a descodificar o caminho oculto da criação literária [...]. A matéria das obras, alquímica ou literária, é a matéria da vida".

[11] "a cosmologia alquímica contém em si uma teoria do ser, uma ontologia".

within themselves, mystically uniting the transcendent with the immanent for the expansion of their own consciousness, the philosopher highlights the dimension of alchemical transmutation in literary language. In this context, each sense can be transfigured, dissolving its original form and meanings.

Hermetic symbols have many names, often contradictory, and exhibit the capacity for renewal, independent of one another. When the Stone is not the Stone, when the rose does not signify a rose, and when the sun is either God or gold, an alchemical poetics and literary alchemy emerge. The mere alchemical significance of symbols evoked in literary works transcends itself. It is "an alchemy that 're-presents' nothing other than the very act of writing itself", as Martin Mees asserts (2019: 158),[12] regarding Nerval's poetic work, finding in it "a Romantic idea inspired by Goethe, considering the poetic work as an exemplary microcosm" (172).[13] The author identifies an alchemical schema parallel to that of poetic creation, not merely as a hermeneutic decoder, within Romantic aesthetics. Indeed, the merchants travelling with Heinrich describe the poet as an organizer of chaotic nature, which, in the alchemical tradition, involves perfecting the imperfect aspects of nature, or the real. Shaping the formless mass of an experience, an idea, or an imagination; calcining it, purifying it, animating it, and perfecting it—this is the work of both alchemy and art.

The process described here highlights the notion that artistic creation, irrespective of genre or medium, parallels the alchemical transformation process. According to Centeno's view, the material of life is equivalent to the material of alchemy and literature, reinforcing this connection. The idea, originating from the uncreated, external to nature, and preceding creation, is initially undifferentiated, akin to what the Orphics referred to as primordial Eros. In this state of tension between opposing forces, what was concentrated expands, dissolves, and transforms. The self and nature might initially separate and

---

[12] "d'une alchimie ne 're-présentant' rien d'autre que le geste propre de l'écriture".

[13] "une idée romantique inspirée de Goethe, considérant l'oeuvre poétique comme un microcosme par excellence".

become opposing forces, eventually reconciling to create a work. This work, emerging from the primordial state, exists in a latent form within the self as a potential seed. Through the tension between the self and the real, this seed is extracted and developed into its final form.

The alchemist-artist acts as a retort, continuously repeating this process as needed for the work. The Philosopher's Stone, representing the completed work, is achieved after discovering and purifying the *prima materia*. However, as previously noted, the process does not end: it undergoes amplification (*amplificatio*), multiplication (*multiplicatio*), and projection (*projectio*). This transmutation involves not only the artist but also the receiver of the art. The reader or audience engages with the work, which affects them in specific ways and influences their own creative processes. This concept aligns with reception theory, suggesting that the recipient becomes part of the creative process through their interaction with the art and the artist.

Language both fixes and recreates the material of alchemy. Alchemy becomes a form of material-memory and creative material. Memory facilitates the transition "from discourse [logos – and thus the rational] to art" (Gadamer 2001: 18).[14] Alchemical texts serve to imprint the memory of various processes and symbols, guiding subsequent alchemists in their pursuits or inspiring future scholars to write about them. Whether oral or written, this memory enables art to recall itself and engage in self-reflection. Alchemical and literary materials are self-reflective. The written word is simultaneously constant and variable; despite its fixed form, it exhibits ontological oscillation, allowing the Shakespearean "to be or not to be" to become a dynamic interplay of existence. The various factors and contexts of its creation render it autonomous and distinct. As for characters, the words that create them alter their lives and consciousnesses—evident in figures like Faust and Heinrich, as well as in Don Quixote or Madame Bovary.

The most skilled alchemist must be able to read, decipher, question, and understand the modes and methods of each symbol, tool and action, externalizing the internal transformation occurring within

---

[14] "do discurso [logos – e, por aí, o racional] à arte".

them. This is also true for the artist, the reader, and the characters and words created, as well as for the work as a whole. Much as in alchemy, this reading and these tools may be internal, reflecting the consciousness of transmutation. When an alchemist considers which path to follow in creating their work—whether the wet path of water or the dry path of fire—they are choosing their method, filtering the necessary operations, and aligning with previous alchemists. Thus, there is no universal list of canonical authors; instead, there are lists according to the intended process. As Manguel (2012: 5) observes, "hierarchy is open to questioning".[15] This idea resonates with Gusmão's assertion (2004: 313) that "the literary relationship can be understood as historical action and interaction or, precisely, as a configuration of the human".[16]

In summary, reading a text through the lens of alchemy involves contemplating the process of becoming, which oscillates between rupture and continuity. This perpetual transmutation, with no indication that perfection is imminent, reflects the fundamental nature of human change. As João Barrento (2011: 121) asserts, "we are at once actors and victims"; we both (re)produce and are (re)produced, (re)present and are (re)presented, leaving our mark on artistic and intellectual creations. If writing has altered our notions of time and space (Manguel 2012: 2), these changes, in turn, affect our literary and worldly perceptions, continually (re)configuring us. The relationship between alchemical and literary matter teaches us that to embrace life fully is to accept our inability to know everything about it, especially concerning art, including alchemical art. It is to reject the idea of a sea of closed, finite answers, constrained by the sands of certainty... The work continues to unfold.

[15] "hierarquia está aberta a questionamento".
[16] "a relação literária pode ser entendida como acção e interacção históricas ou, precisamente, configuração do humano".

REFERENCES

ADELUNG, Johann Christopher (1798). *Grammatisch-kritisches Wörterbuch der hochdeutschen Mundart mit beständiger Vergleichung der übrigen Mundarten, besonders aber der Oberdeutschen.* Vol. III. Leipzig: Breitkopf und Härtel.

AGAMBEN, Giorgio (2017). *The Fire and the Tale* (trans. Lorenzo Chiesa). Redwood City: Stanford University Press.

ALLERT, Beate (2004). "Romanticism and the Visual Arts", in *The Camden House History of German Literature*, vol. 8, *The Literature of German Romanticism* (ed. Dennis Mahoney). Rochester: Camden House, pp. 273-306.

AMO, Castro del; CERRO, Elena Fernandez de; PANIAGUA, Victoria; ZABLBIDEA, Victor (1980). *Alquimia y ocultismo* (trans. Teresa Carrilho). Lisbon: Edições 70.

ANDREAE, Johann Valentin (1973). *Fama Fraternitatis (1614). Confessio Fraternitatis. (1615). Chymische Hochzeit: Christiani Rosenkreutz. Anno 1459 (1616)* (ed. Richard van Dülmen). Stuttgart: Calwer.

BACHELARD, Gaston (1986). *La psychanalyse du feu.* Paris: Gallimard.

_____ (1988). *Fragments d'une poétique du feu.* Paris: Presses Universitaires de France.

BALCAROVÁ, Markéta (2016). "Die Schlange als Reflexionsmittel in den Künstlertexten der deutschen Romantik". Ph.D. thesis in German Studies. Prague: Karlova University. https://is.cuni.cz/webapps/zzp/detail/104964/.

BARRENTO, João (2011). *O Mundo está cheio de Deuses. Crise e crítica do contemporâneo.* Lisbon: Assírio & Alvim.

BEESE, Marianne (2000). *Novalis. Leben und Werk.* Rostock: Neuer Hochschulschriftenverlag.

149

BENDER, Cora; HENSEL, Thomas, SCHÜTTPELZ, Erhard (eds.) (2007). *Schlangenritual. Der Transfer der Wissensformen vom Tsu'ti'kive der Hopi bis zu Aby Warburgs Kreuzlinger Vortrag.* Berlin: Akademie Verlag.

BERTHELOT, Marcellin (1887). *Collection des anciennes texts grecs.* Livre I. Paris: Georges Steinheil.

BEUTIN, Wolfgang; EHLERT; EMMERICH, Wolfgang; HOFFACKER, Helmut; LUTZ, Bernd; MEID, Volker; SCHNELL, Ralf; STEIN, Peter; STEPHAN, Inge (1993). *A History of German Literature: From the Beginnings to the Present Day* (trans. Clare Krojzl). London and New York: Routledge.

_____ (1888). _____. Livres II et III. Paris: Georges Steinheil.

BOHM, Arnd (2004). "Goethe and the Romantics", in *The Camden House History of German Literature,* vol. 8, *The Literature of German Romanticism* (ed. Dennis Mahoney). Rochester: Camden House, pp. 35-60.

BÖHME, Jacob (1911). *The Forty Questions of the Soul and The Clavis* (trans. John Sparrow). London: John M. Watkins.

_____. (1991). *The Key* (trans. William Law). Grand Rapids: Phanes Press.

_____ (2013). *Aurora (Morgen Röte im Aufgang); Mysterium Pansophicum* (ed. Marco Pasi). Leiden: Brill.

BONARDEL, Françoise (2002). *La voie hermétique.* Paris: Dervy.

BRION, Marcel (1962). *L'Allemagne romantique.* Vol. II. Paris: Albin Michel.

BURCKHARDT, Titus (1991). *Alquimia: significado e imagem do mundo* (trans. Emanuel Lourenço Godinho). Lisbon: Dom Quixote.

CENTENO, Yvette K. (1976). *A simbologia alquímica no conto da serpente verde de Goethe.* Lisbon: Universidade Nova de Lisboa.

_____ (1983). *A alquimia e o Fausto de Goethe.* Lisbon: Arcádia.

_____ (1987). *Literatura e alquimia. Ensaios.* Lisbon: Editorial Presença.

_____ (1991). *A arte de jardinar. Do símbolo no texto literário.* Lisbon: Editorial Presença.

CERONETTI, Guido (1993). *The silence of the body: Materials for the study of medicine* (trans. Michael Moore). New York: Harper Collins.

CORNFORND, F. M. (1975). *Principium sapientae. As origens do pensamento filosófico grego* (trans. Maria Manuela Rocheta Santos). Lisbon: Fundação Calouste Gulbenkian.

DELBOS, Victor (2017). *O problema moral na filosofia de Spinoza e na história do spinozismo*. Rio de Janeiro: FGV.

DODDS, Eric Robertson (1997). *The Greeks and the irrational.* Berkeley: University of California Press.

DOHM, Burkhard (2000). *Poetische Alchemie. Öffnung zur Sinnlichkeit in der Hohelied- und Bibeldichtung von der protestantischen Barockmystik bis zum Pietismus.* Tübingen: Niemeyer.

DURAND, Gilbert (1969). *Les structures anthropologiques de l'imaginaire.* Paris: Bordas.

DYE, Ellis (2004). *Love and Death in Goethe:One and Double.* Rochester: Camden House.

ECKERMANN, Johann Peter (2013). *Gespräche mit Goethe in den letzten Jahren seines Lebens.* Paderborn: Großdruckbuch.

ELIADE, Mircea (1952). *Images et symboles. Essai sur le symbolisme magico-religieux.* Paris: Gallimard.

EVOLA, Julius (2006). *La tradizione ermetica. Nei suoi simboli, nella sua dottrina e nella sua "Arte Regia".* Rome: Edizioni Mediterranee.

FABRE, M. Pierre Jean (2009). *L'Abregé des Secrets Chymiques.* Cortaillod: Arbre d'Or.

FIGUEIRA, Dorothy Mathilde (1991). *Translating the Orient: The Reception of Shakuntala in Nineteenth-Century Europe.* Albany: State University of New York Press.

FLAMEL, Nicolas (2012). *Le bréviaire de Nicolas Flamel d'après un manuscrit.* Geneva: Arbre d'Or.

GADAMER, H. G (2001). *Elogio da Teoria* (trans. J. T. Proença). Lisbon: Edições 70.

GEBELEIN, Helmut. *Alchemie.* Munich: Diederichs, 2000.

GOETHE, Johann Wolfgang von (1829). *Goethes Werke.* Band 13. Tübingen: Cotta'sche Verlagsbuchhandlung.

_____ (1901). *Goethe und Lavater.* Band 16, (ed. Heinrich Funck). Weimar: Verlag der Goethe-Gesellschaft.

_____ (1963). *Gedichte.* Weimar: Volksverlag.

_____ (2010). *Faust* (ed. Erich Trunz). Munich: C. H. Beck.

_____ (2016). *Zur Farbenlehre*. Berlin: Hofenberg.

GRAY, Ronald Douglas (2010). *Goethe, the Alchemist: A Study of Alchemical Symbolism in Goethe's Literary and Scientific Works*. Cambridge: Cambridge University Press.

GUSMÃO, Manuel (2004). "Da literatura enquanto configuração histórica do humano", in *Actas do Colóquio Internacional de Literatura e História*, vol. I. Porto: Faculdade de Letras da Universidade do Porto, pp. 309-319.

HALLUM, Benjamin (2008). *Zosimus Arabus. The Reception of Zosimus of Panopolis in the Arabic/Islamic World*. Ph.D. thesis in Combined Historical Studies. London: University of London.

HELFER, Martha B. (2004). "Gender Studies and Romanticism", in *The Camden House History of German Literature*, vol. 8, *The Literature of German Romanticism* (ed. Dennis Mahoney). Rochester: Camden House, pp. 229-250.

HERRERO, Miguel de Jáuregui (2010). *Orphism and the Christianity in late Antiquity* (trans. Jennifer Ottman and Daniel Rodriguez). Berlin: De Gruyter.

HILL, David (ed.) (2003). *Literature of the Sturm und Drang*, vol. 6, *The Camden House History of German Literature*. Rochester: Camden House.

HILLMAN, James (2008). *A blue fire*. London and New York: Routledge.

_____ (2010). *Alchemical Psychology*. Thompson, CT: Spring Publications.

HOLMYARD, E. J. (2012). *Alchemy*. New York: Dover Publications.

HOFFMEISTER, Gerhart (2004). "From Goethe's *Wilhelm Meister* to anti-*Meister* Novels: The Romantic Novel between Tieck's *William Lovell* and Hoffmann's *Kater Murr*", in *The Camden House History of German Literature*, vol. 8, *The Literature of German Romanticism* (ed. Dennis Mahoney). Rochester: Camden House, pp. 79-100.

HU, Yihong (2007). *Unterwegs zum Roman. Novalis' Werdegang als Übergang von der Philosophie zur Poesie*. Paderborn: Schöningh.

JUNG, Carl Gustav (1963). *Gesammelte Werke*. Vol. 11. *Zur Psychologie westlicher und östlicher Religion*. Zürich: Rascher.

_____ (1972). *Gesammelte Werke*. Vol. 12. *Psychologie und Alchemie*.

Zürich: Rachser.

_____ (1976). *Gesammelte Werke*. Vol. 9. *Die Archetypen und das kollektive Unbewusste*. Olten und Freiburg im Breisgau: Walter-Verlag.

_____ (1977). *Mysterium Coniunctionis: an Inquiry into the Separation and Synthesis of Psychic Opposites in Alchemy* (trans. R. F. C. Hull). Princeton: Princeton University Press.

_____ (ed.) (1979). *Der Mensch und seine Symbole*. Michigan: Melsa Verlag.

_____ (1981). *Gesammelte Werke*. Vol. 18. Part. II. *Das symbolische Leben*. Brisgóvia: Walter-Verlag.

_____ (1988). *Aion: estudos sobre o simbolismo do Si-mesmo* (trans. Mateus Ramalho). Rio de Janeiro: Ed. Vozes.

_____ (1990). *Gesammelte Werke*. Vol. 14. Part. I *Mysterium Coniunctionis*. Olten und Freiburg im Breisgau: Walter-Verlag.

_____ (1991). *Psicologia e Alquimia* (trans. Maria Luiza Appy, Margaret Makray, Dora Mariana Ribeiro Ferreira da Silva). Rio de Janeiro: Ed. Vozes.

KIRCHWEGER, Anton (2016). *Golden Chain Homeri*. Vol II. Part. I. San Jose: AMORC.

KUZNIAR, Alice (1992). "Hearing Women's Voices in Heinrich von Ofterdingen", in *PMLA*, Vol. 107, No. 5 (Oct), pp. 1196-1207.

LEMBERT, Alexandra (2004). *The Heritage of Hermes*: *Alchemie in Contemporary Britisch Literature*. Berlin: Galda & Wilch.

LIEDTKE, Ralf (1996). *Die Hermetik traditionelle Philosophie der Differenz*. Paderborn: Ferdinand Schöningh Verlag.

_____ (2003). *Das romantische Paradigma der Chemie Friedrich von Hardenbergs Naturphilosophie zwischen Empirie und alchemistischer Spekulation*. Paderborn: Mentis.

LINDSAY, Jack (1970). *The origins of alchemy in graeco-roman Egypt*. New York: Barnes & Noble.

LITTLEJOHNS, Richard (2004). "Early Romanticism", in *The Camden House History of German Literature*, vol. 8, *The Literature of German Romanticism* (ed. Dennis Mahoney). Rochester: Camden House, pp. 61-77.

LOURENÇO, Frederico (trans.) (2018). *Bíblia* (vol. I). *Novo*

Testamento: os quatro Evangelhos. Lisbon: Quetzal.

MAHONEY, Dennis F. (ed.) (2004). *The Literature of German Romanticism*. Vol. 8. *The Camden House History of German Literature*. Rochester: Camden House.

MÄHL, Hans-Joachim (1967). "Goethes Urteil über Novalis. Ein Beitrag zur Geschichte der Kritik an der deutschen Romantik", in *Jahrbuch des Freien Deutschen Hochstifts*. Tübingen: Max Niemeyer Verlag, pp. 130-270.

_____ (1994). *Die Idee des goldenen Zeitalters im Werk des Novalis*. Tübingen: Max Niemeyer.

MANGUEL, Alberto (2002). "O temor ao poder do leitor continua", in *Ler* (Nov). Lisbon: Círculo de Leitores, pp. 2-11.

MARQUES, Manuela de Sousa (1947). "O romantismo em Novalis", in *Revista da faculdade de letras*, tomo XIII – 2ª série, nº2, pp. 44-52.

MARTENSEN, HANS LASSEN (1885). *Jacob Bohme: His Life and Teaching or Studies in Theosophy* (trans. Thomas Rhys Evans). London: Hodder and Stoughton.

MARTÍNEZ, Francisco Albarracín (2016). "Ramón Llull: arte y mística. Imágenes, memoria y dignidades", in *El azufre rojo*, III. Murcia: Universidad de Murcia, pp. 221-240.

MARX, Adolf Bernhard (1902). *Ludwig van Beethoven Leben und Schaffen*. Leipzig: Gebrüder Reinecke.

MEES, Martin (2019). "L'alchimie romantique de la Forme. Création et puissance poétiques chez Nerval", in *Les formes romantiques de la vie. Poétisations de l'existence dans le romantisme européen*, (ed. Laure Cahen-Maurel, Victoire Feuillebois and Martin Mees). Paris: Hermann, pp. 155-186.

MEIER, Michael (2007). *Michael Meiers Chymisches Cabinet. Atalanta fugiens deutsch nach der Ausgabe von 1708* (trans. Thomas Hofmeier). Berlin: Thurneysser, 2007.

MICHAUD, Guy (1961). *Méssage poétique du symbolisme*. Paris: Nizet.

MICHELET, Émile (1890). *De l'ésotérisme dans l'art*. Paris: G. Carré.

MOLNÁR, Géza von (1987). *Romantic Vision, Ethical Context: Novalis and Artistic Autonomy*. Minneapolis: University of Minnesota Press.

NAVARRO, Alejandro Martín (2020). "Viaje místico hacia lo Uno. Estudio comparativo sobre sufismo y Romanticismo"; in *Thémata, Revista de Filosofía*, nº62, pp. 125-142.

NIETZSCHE, Friedrich (1907). *Die Geburt der Tragödie*. Leipzig: C. G. Naumann Verlag.

NOVALIS (1942). *Henri d'Ofterdingen* (trans. Marcel Camus). Paris: Aubier.

_____. (1945). *Gesammelte Werke*, Vol. I (ed. Carl Seelig). Zürich: Bühl.

_____ (1945b). _____, Vol. II (ed. Carl Seelig). Zürich: Bühl.

_____ (1946). _____, Vol. III (ed. Carl Seelig). Zürich: Bühl.

_____ (1946b). _____, Vol. IV (ed. Carl Seelig). Zürich: Bühl.

_____ (1946c). _____, Vol. V (ed. Carl Seelig). Zürich: Bühl.

_____ (1960). *Novalis Schriften* (ed. Paul Kluckhohn and Richard Samuel), Band: *Das philosophische Werk*, vol. I. Estugarda: W. Kohlhammer.

_____ (1982). *Himnos a la Noche. Enrique de Ofterdingen* (trans. Eustaquio Barjau). Barcelona: Ediciones Orbis S. A.

OLIVEIRA, Rafael Guimarães Abras (2014). "Poesia infinita: o problema estético em Novalis". Master's dissertation in Aesthetics and Philosophy of Art. Ouro Preto: Institute of Philosophy, Arts, and Culture, Federal University of Ouro Preto.

PANNO, Giovanni (2005). "Urkönig-Urmenscg: il romanticismo politico di novalis ed il katechon del re", in *Ethic@ - An International Journal for Moral Philosophy*, 4 (1), pp. 55–81.

PARACELSO (1894). *The Hermetic and Alchemical Writings of Aureolus Philippus Theophrastus Bombast, of Hohenheim, called Paracelso the Great*. Vol. I (trans. Arthur Edward Waite). London: James Elliott and Co.

_____. (1976). _____. Vol. II (trans. Arthur Edward Waite). London: James Elliott and Co.

_____ (2008). *Paracelso (Theophrastus Bombastus von Hohenheim, 1493–1541)* (trans. Andrew Weeks). Leiden: Brill.

PESSOA, Fernando (1982). *Livro do Desassossego por Bernardo Soares* (ed. Jacinto do Prado Coelho). Lisbon: Ática.

PIMENOV, Alexei (2020). *German Nationalism and Indian Political*

Thought. The Influence of Ancient Indian Philosophy on the German Romantics. London and New York: Routledge.

PLATÃO (2000). *Fedro ou da Beleza* (trans. Pinharanda Gomes). Lisbon: Guimarães Editores.

PRAGER, Debra N (2014). *The German Literary Encounter with the Eastern Other*. Rochester: Boydell & Brewer.

PRINCIPE, Lawrence M. (2013). *The secrets of alchemy*. Chicago: University of Chicago Press.

RAMPLING, Jennifer (2014). "Eine geheime Sprache. Die Ripley-Bildrollen", in *Kunst und Alchemie. Das Geheimnis der Verwandlung* (ed. Sven Dupré). Munich: Hirmer, pp. 38-57.

ROMMEL, Gabriele (ed.) (1998). *Geheimnisvolle Zeichen: Alchemie, Magie, Mystik und Natur bei Novalis*. Leipzig: Edition Leipzig.

_____ (2004). "Romanticism and Natural Science", in *The Camden House History of German Literature*, vol. 8, *The Literature of German Romanticism* (ed. Dennis Mahoney). Rochester: Camden House, pp.209-228.

ROOB, Alexander (2006). *O museu hermético: alquimia e misticismo* (trans. Tersa Curvelo). Cologne: Taschen.

SAMUELS, Andrew (1999). *Jung e os pós junguianos* (trans. Eva Lucia Salm. Rio de Janeiro: Imago.

SCHEFER, Olivier (2001). *Poésie de l'infini. Novalis et la question esthétique*. Brussels: La Lettre volée.

_____ (2005). *Résonances du Romantisme*. Brussels: La Lèttre volée.

SCHLEGEL, Friedrich (1803). *Europa: eine Zeitschrift*. Vol. I. Frankfurt: Friedrich Wilmans.

_____. (1958): *Kritische Friedrich-Schlegel-Ausgabe* (ed. Ernst Behler). Erste und zweite Abteilung. Zürich: Thomas Verlag.

SCHLEGEL, August Wilhelm, SCHLEGEL, Friedrich (1960). *Athenaeum (1798-1800)*. Stuttgart: J. G. Cotta'sche Verlagsbuchhandlung.

SCHMIEDER, Karl Christoph (2005). *Die Geschichte der Alchemie*. Wiesbaden: Marix Verlag.

SCHOLEM, Gerschom (2001). *Ursprung und Anfänge der Kabbala*. Berlin: De Gruyter.

_____. (2015). *Alchimia e Kabbalah* (tr. Maria Sartorio). Milan: SE.

SCHULZ, Gerhard (2004). "From "Romantick" to "Romantic": The Genesis of German Romanticism in Late Eighteenth-Century Europe", in *The Camden House History of German Literature*, vol. 8, *The Literature of German Romanticism* (ed. Dennis Mahoney). Rochester: Camden House, pp. 25-34.

SCHÜTT, Hans-Werner (2000). *Auf der Suche nach dem Stein der Weisen. Die Geschichte der Alchemie*. Munich: Beck.

SPEIGTH, Allen (2020). "Early German Romanticism and Literature: Goethe, Schlegel, Novalis and the New Philosophical Importance of the Novel", in *The Palgrave Handbook of German Romantic Philosophy* (ed. Elizabeth Millán Brusslan). Chicago: Palgrave Macmillan, pp. 297-316.

STROE, Mihai A (2007). "The Alchemy of Romanticism in Scientific Context", in *B. A. S.: British and American Studies*, 13. Timişoara: Editura Universităţii de Vest din Timişoara / Diacritic Timisoara, pp. 61-76.

SZULAKOWSKA, Urszula (2017). *The Alchemical Virgin Mary in the Religious and Political Context of the Renaissance*. Newcastle upon Tyne: Cambridge Scholars Publishing.

THAPAR, Romila (2011). *Shakuntala: Texts, Readings, Histories*. New York: Columbia University Press.

UERLINGS, Herbert (1991). *Friedrich von Hardenberg, genannt Novalis. Werk und Forschung*. Stuttgart: Metzler.

ULMANNUS (1983). *Buch der Heiligen Dreifaltigkeit*. Cologne: Instituts für Geschichte der Medizin.

UŽDAVINYS, Algis (2011). *Orpheus and the roots of Platonism*. London: The Matheson Trust.

VALENTINE, Basil (2016). *Last Will and Testament*. San Jose: AMORC.

VAUGHAN, Thomas [Eugenius Philalethes] (1919). *The works of Thomas Vaughan. Eugenius Philalethes* (trans. Arthur Edward Waite). London: Thesophical Publishing House.

VERNANT, Jean-Pierre (1990). *Mythe et religion en Grèce ancienne*. Paris: Éditions du Seuil.

WALSH, David (1983). *The Mysticism of Innerworldly Fulfillment: A Study of Jacob Boehme*. Gainesville: University Presses of Florida.

WEBER, Johannes (2013). *Goethe und die Jungen. Über die Grenzen der Poesie und vom Vorrang des wirklichen Lebens*. Berlin: De Gruyter.

WELLING, Georg von (2006). *Opus Mago-Cabbalisticum et Theosophicum* (trans. Joseph G. McVeigh). San Francisco: Red Wheel/ Weiser.

WITTKOWSKI, Wolfgang (ed.) (1986). *Verlorene Klassik? Ein Symposium*. Tübingen: Max Niemeyer Verlag.

YATES, Frances (1964). *Giordano Bruno and the hermetic tradition*. London: Routledge.

www.ingramcontent.com/pod-product-compliance
Lightning Source LLC
Chambersburg PA
CBHW052141170626
46812CB00004B/1530